Lake Effect

Ronald W. Adams

PublishAmerica
Baltimore

© 2003 by Ronald W. Adams.
All rights reserved. No part of this book may be reproduced in any form without written permission from the publishers, except by a reviewer who may quote brief passages in a review to be printed in a newspaper or magazine.

First printing

ISBN: 1-59286-745-6
PUBLISHED BY PUBLISHAMERICA BOOK
PUBLISHERS
www.publishamerica.com
Baltimore

Printed in the United States of America

For Trish, Danny, and Katie

Prologue

Sharon Dellaplante pushed the double stroller through the slushy snow in the mall parking lot. The loaded bags of clothes and toys dangled in front of her from a small hook she hung from the strollers handle. Her son, David, sat in the front seat and stuck his tongue out to catch snowflakes as they fell gently from the frigid December night sky. Sarah, her baby, sat in the rear, her eyes and nose the only things visible from beneath her winter clothes. A gust of wind coupled with a patch of black ice to provide some additional excitement as they made their way to their minivan.

She pulled the stroller to the driver's side of the van, using the keyfob remote to unlock the doors. She pulled her jacket sleeve up and her glove down to glance at her watch. It was almost ten o'clock, way past the kids' bedtime. She cursed herself, and Christmas, under her breath as she unhooked David from the stroller and urged him to climb up into his car seat. She repeated the process for Sarah, only placing her in the seat first and strapping her in. She finished getting David settled, and produced two sippy-cups of chocolate milk for them to enjoy on the ride home. On a good night, it might take them 45 minutes to get home. This night, well who knew. The kids would be asleep before they got home.

Sharon closed the door against the winter chill, and pushed the stroller and all the presents to the back of the van. She lifted the rear gate and put the presents and the stroller inside. Carefully, she made her way back to the driver's side door when she felt herself being grabbed roughly from behind. Survival instinct took over and she brought the heel of her boot down hard against what she assumed was her attacker's shin, scraping along the bone as she jammed into their foot. She heard a shout of pain, followed by the release of her arms as the man fell backwards momentarily. She bolted forward.

A second man came at her from around the front of the man, his face covered by what looked like a ski mask. He swung fast and hard, and hit her shoulder and spun her sideways against the snow and the slush. She felt the freezing wetness spread against the heat of her panic. She tried to stand up, and was grabbed again by the first man. He was about to take his painful shin out on her, but the other one shouted to him from the open driver's door, "Dump the bitch! We just want the ride."

At that she felt herself being lifted and tossed like a rag doll over one of the snow banks that lined the parking lot, landing hard on her back and sliding down away from her car. She heard the men shouting and laughing, then the motor turning over. She flipped herself up and on to her feet, scrambling up the short icy slope in time to see the van lurch backward, then forward again and away.

"David!" she screamed through the nearly empty parking lot. "Sarah!"

One

I woke up early Sunday morning, just after Christmas, and came downstairs to get the coffee going. I am a man of very few vices, but coffee is one of them. The fresh smell of that first cup in the morning, which the Folger's coffee people say is the best part of waking up, is more than a morning ritual, and not quite a way of life. Stumbling through an early morning brain fog, I went to the kitchen, got down the filters and the coffee and made myself a pot. Turning on the baby monitors next, I listened intently to the sounds of Kyle and Amanda sleeping. There is nothing quite like the gentle sound babies make when they breathe, and the little rustling sounds as they turn over. Maybe because of my line of work as a private investigator, I get to see the ugly side of humanity on an all too frequent basis. Or maybe because I became a father relatively late, but even a year after we adopted the two of them, I still love listening to the wee small baby noises, the chatter with their toys, the way the sheets sound as they begin to stir. It's security to me, an oasis in the midst of some of the less pleasant things I have to do. I have loved music all my life, and I still don't believe I have ever heard anything sweeter than those sounds. Chopin would be jealous.

When the coffee was done, I poured myself the first cup of the day. I took it into the family room, which, since Santa Claus came for a visit, looks like a post-apocalyptic Toys 'R' Us, and turned on the television to catch the early news. It was a morning routine that brought some measure of normalcy and connection, like the feeling somewhere there is another dad out there, listening to his kids, drinking his coffee, and catching up on the news of his world. Most of it was bad; most of it affected me very little. And, to be fair, my attention was divided between the newsperson telling me about the latest terrorist attempts to smuggle a bomb into the US from Canada, and the sounds of my 20-month-old daughter babbling stories to the stuffed toys in her crib. I was about to get up to get my next cup of coffee, when a local story hit me between the eyes.

The woman reporter was standing at the shore of Lake Erie, the gray dawn sky behind her serving as a grim backdrop to the story. She was telling the camera about Hamburg Police and Erie County Sheriff's Department fishing out a minivan from the boat launch in the section of Hamburg known as Locksley Park. Locksley Park is one of those lakeside neighborhoods with houses located on one side of the street and Lake Erie located on the other. The area is incredibly picturesque, with sails visible on the summer horizon, and in the winter the frozen lake looks like an arctic tundra. To the west, you get spectacular sunsets, and to the east, the mighty Buffalo skyline.

The van had been reported stolen a couple of nights before, carjacked from the Galleria Mall in Cheektowaga from a woman who said she had just finished Christmas shopping when she put her two babies in their car seats. The woman said she was struck from behind by some black youths, and that they stole her van with her children and their Christmas presents still inside. The reporter then told the camera about the grim discovery of the van with the bodies of two small children, one boy and one girl, along with several bags of toys. At this time, the reporter said, police have no suspects, and the investigation is continuing. I turned off the television, thought of my own two babies upstairs, looked at the toys strewn across the room, and choked back a tear as Amanda called out, "Dadda!"

I put my cup on the kitchen counter, and quietly slipped upstairs to get her. It was my turn to let my wife sleep in, which meant getting the kids up and getting them breakfast. I don't mind doing it at all, especially since Paula has them when I'm at work. Ever since we adopted Kyle and Amanda about a year ago, Paula has given up her career to take care of them as a full time stay-at-home mom. The least I can do is give her a weekend morning or two off. So I got Amanda up first, changed her, and set her down in the family room with Sesame Street. Kyle was next, and he gave me a prize-winning smile when I entered his room to get him out of his crib. Diaper changed, in to see Sesame Street, and Kyle was ready to start the day. In the meantime, I started breakfast, and thanked God that two year olds were relatively easy to please. Two pieces of toast with

LAKE EFFECT

grape jelly, two glasses of chocolate milk, and an apple cut and dipped in cinnamon sugar, and we have breakfast made for the king and queen of the castle. I set them in their high chairs, gave them their plates, and proceeded with the mundane tasks of getting the day started.

As I was emptying the dishwasher, clinking dishes and glasses around, my mind wandered back to the two kids in the minivan, strapped into their car seats. Did they say how old they were? Were there any other marks on the bodies? Is there an autopsy report ready yet? The official documents would state the cause of death as apparent drowning, but was it really that simple, I wondered. The more I thought about them, the more upset I was becoming. Paula snuck up behind me and kissed me gently on the cheek as I was finishing with the dishes, and that broke my funk. Good things happen when she kisses me, so I look forward to every one of them.

"You look way too grumpy this morning," she teased, smiling. Her hair was still wet from the shower, and smelled clean and fresh and faintly of flowers.

"Feeling grumpy, but I'll get over it," I replied.

"You better, mister. I have no intention of spending your day off trying to figure out what wild hair is getting to you. You have just got to lighten up."

"I will. It's still early and I haven't had near enough coffee," I cracked.

She walked into the family room and kissed the kids good morning. "I am going to keep you from watching Elmo, if this is the way you behave." Paula had a way with a threat.

"Yeah, yeah, yeah," I said. "How about breakfast?"

Paula began getting breakfast ready and I cleaned up the kids and the after-breakfast mess they made. Amanda and Kyle took off to the family room to wreak havoc there, and I went back to the kitchen table to finish my coffee. Paula brought over a plate with bacon, eggs, home fries, and toast, and it smelled too good to let get cold. I watched her as she cleaned up the kitchen. It amazes me after 15 years of marriage how she still manages to look so good first thing in the morning. Her dark hair just above her shoulders, her limitless grace at the most commonplace tasks, and the way her eyes just draw me in. I fell in love with those eyes so long ago, and never stopped falling.

After I finished, I gave Paula a kiss and a smile, and went up to take a shower. I let the hot water beat on my neck and back, and it felt really good. I let my thoughts fall back to the two kids strapped in the van, and I could see them, water slowly rising inside as the van dropped deeper into the lake. It was mid-winter in western New York, so the water would have been icy cold. Were they awake? Maybe. Did they know what was happening? Hard to say, except that they probably began to panic as the water reached their legs, and struggled to get out of their car seats. As the water reached their chins they were probably crying, calling out, until it enveloped them. They more than likely took in huge lungfuls of water instead of air as they screamed, until they finally suffocated. I felt a chill in my spine as these thoughts blasted in my mind, my concentration interrupted only by my wife knocking on the bathroom door.

"Joe? Are you alive in there?" she called. " I have been trying to get your attention. Kevin Garner's on the phone for you."

I shut the water off, and grabbed a towel to wipe my face. Paula handed me the phone through the shower door. "Kevin," I said. "Long time, no hear, what can I do for you?"

"Hey, Joe." Kevin and I had been friends since college. He was an adjuster and investigator for Kellerman Life Insurance Company, so our paths continued to cross from time to time. He was a friendly, likeable guy, and I enjoyed dealing with him when I did. "Am I catching you at a bad time?"

He sounded more serious than I had heard him in a while. "Just getting out of the shower, Kev. To what do I owe the pleasure?"

"Did you hear about the van they fished out by you last night?"

"Yeah. I saw it on the news this morning."

"Any thoughts?"

"Yeah," I said angrily. "I think it sucks. I think whoever did it knew the kids were back there, and then ditched it in the water

LAKE EFFECT

anyway. Why?"

"Kellerman Insurance had a policy on each of the kids, kinda big, too. They asked me to look into it, and I told them I needed you."

"Beneficiary?" I asked.

"Mother is listed as primary, and her father is listed as secondary."

"Really?" That seemed odd. Why not the kids' father, I wondered.

"Yup. Interested?" Kevin asked.

"Yeah, I'll take it," I told him.

"Can you meet me at the Circle Diner for lunch?"

"What time?"

"How about noon?"

"Let's make it 12:30, Kev. That way I can help Paula with lunch and getting the kids down for a nap."

"See you at 12:30, Joe."

"Okay, Kevin, see ya soon."

I hung up the phone, dried off and got dressed. I went downstairs, where Paula was just finishing loading the dishwasher. She turned to look at me, sullen and a little upset. "He's never called you at home on a Sunday unless it was to play golf. He's got a case for you, doesn't he?" she asked.

"Yeah," I said. "He wants to meet me for lunch, and I told him it would keep until naptime."

Paula was jealous of my time spent on the job, especially on the weekend. She hated that it took me away from her and the kids. So did I. "You don't expect me to like this, working on your day off, do you?"

"I don't, so why should you? But Kevin and I go back a long way, and if he needs to see me today, I'm pretty sure it's important. Besides, if his bosses at Kellerman think it's important enough to call him on a Sunday, then we should meet. You understand investigation work, hon. I have to take it when it comes around. And working for an insurance company means we'll be getting paid real money, on time, for a change." I was rationalizing for my own sake as well as for hers. But more for her, because there was a part of me that truly wanted to find out what happened to those two little kids.

"Alright," Paula sighed. "If I have to give you up today, at least tell me the basics."

"Seen the news yet today? The story of the little boy and girl in the van?"

"Oh God, I did, Joe. They were in a car or van or something when it was carjacked around Christmas. Is that the case he wants you for?"

"Apparently, Kellerman Insurance held a life insurance policy on the two of them, with the mother and her father named as beneficiaries. Kevin says the amount is pretty large, so they need to check into it before they pay out."

"Is there something unusual about the policy, besides the amount?"

"I'm not sure, and Kevin didn't say just now. I guess that's why they want me to look into it with him."

"Are you going to be gone all day?" Paula asked, hopeful of the right answer.

"Don't see why I would be, hon. I'm just gonna meet with Kevin, go over the ground rules I guess, and won't really get into until Monday. I should be home before the kids get up from their nap." I thought to myself that there is probably not enough to really get started with until the beginning of the week, when all the autopsy and forensics are in to the police. "I'll be back before you miss me."

"That long?" Paula teased, smiling.

Two

Kevin Garner was ten minutes late, which was actually as close to on time as he has ever been. I liked to refer to this as the "Garner Factor". The Garner factor dictates that whenever Kevin has to be somewhere for a meeting, you add 15 to 30 minutes to the actual start time to allow for late phone calls, traffic, fast food stops, and assorted other excuses. I was drinking my coffee when Kevin came in. I stood so he could see me at the side booth, and he nodded.

Kevin was a stocky man, not quite six foot tall and not quite fat, just built squarely. He had a shock of strawberry blonde hair, peppered with a little more gray than he used to have, and very friendly, almost smiling gray-green eyes. He was Old First Ward from South Buffalo, a friendly Irish guy that was as comfortable at a pub as he was in a boardroom. I met Kevin in college in Buffalo. We developed an instant friendship, being from similar neighborhoods in different cities. As the new kid on campus from South Boston, Kevin took me under his wing and properly introduced me to life in the Queen City. Some lessons I remembered very well, some were a little hazier. We shared a lot of the same interests, philosophies, and taste in beer and coffee. The only difference was, I had a sense of time, and he never did.

"Jeez, Joe, it's good to see you. How's Paula and the kids?" asked Kevin as he stuck his thick hand out to shake mine.

"Great, thanks Kev. How's everything at the Garner House?" I asked, more to be polite.

"Terrific. We gotta get together before spring hits and have dinner. Amy keeps asking me to ask you."

"We will, Kev. So talk to me, tell me about this case."

"My company's concerned about this one, Joe. They're concerned because the amount is a bit excessive for two little kids. The executives don't mind collecting the money on the big premiums, especially because you're talking about two kids, and the long life they are supposed to have ahead of them. That makes it extremely profitable. But when things like this happen, they get nervous and jerky. That, and the fact that they think they aren't satisfied with the investigation by the cops. They want me to dig into it, make sure everything is as clean as it can be, and I need your help to do it." Kevin's eyes got cold fast. "This one's not right, ya know what I mean?"

"Yeah," I said. "I didn't like it when I heard it on TV, I liked it less when you called. Why would someone take the chance on a murder rap by dumping those kids in the water with the van? If all they wanted was the stuff in the van, or the van itself, why not call the cops after they take out what they wanted, and let the kids live. Odds are, if this was a real carjacking they would still be alive. The way I see it, they knew the kids were there, and that means they meant to kill them."

"Or that the assholes panicked and dumped it in the water without thinking," said Kevin.

"Possible," I said, "but not likely. But this still sounds like something that the local cops could handle, and you can wrap up whatever loose ends without hiring me."

The waitress came over with more fresh coffee. She filled my cup, and offered it to Kevin. "Hi, I'm Cheri, and I'll be your waitress. Can I get you guys anything?" she asked.

I motioned I was sticking with the coffee, and Kevin ordered a fried bacon, egg, and cheese sandwich, an order of fries and a chocolate milkshake. I considered commenting about keeping his girlish figure, but then thought the better of it.

"There are some other factors in this, Joe," Kevin said. "There are a lot of things that enter into the equation that could be misconstrued as improper. For one thing, I am close to the family. My family has known the Dellaplantes for years. And for another, the CEO of Kellerman Insurance and the grandfather of the two babies are on the same charitable boards, same church groups, it could get messy. And polite society, even here, hates messes."

I thought about that, and how I hated politics affecting the truth. To be honest, I found the two concepts to be mutually exclusive, so to be told I was to be used to keep the politics out of the truth had its

LAKE EFFECT

appeal. Anyway, I liked Kevin, and his family, and I could use the work.

"So tell me what you know, Kevin" I said, and sipped the hot coffee.

Kevin pulled out a file folder from his briefcase, took a deep breath, and began slowly. "The deceased are David Dellaplante, age 2 ½ years, and his sister Sarah, eighteen months. Preliminary cause of death, according to the M.E. at the scene, was asphyxiation from water. The van was pulled from the water off the boat launch, nose first on its driver's side as they dragged it. Looks like they rolled backwards down the ramp, and the wind and waves pushed it over once it filled with water." Kevin fell silent, as he continued to review the documents in his file folder. His voice was beginning to crack a little, but he pulled it back together by clearing his throat. I could tell he was beginning to think about his own four kids at home.

"Will I get a look at this file, too?" I asked.

"Of course, Joe, whatever you need," he said, sliding a folder my way.

The waitress returned a few minutes later with our order. I drank my coffee while Kevin started in on his sandwich. I pulled the folder towards me to get a closer look at the details. I read it quietly as Kevin ate. I turned the pages, soaking in what little details they offered. "What do you think, Kevin?"

Kevin took a bite of his sandwich, politely wiped his mouth, and started. "What I think, Joe, is that the kids were dead before they hit the water. I think the whole van in the water thing was just meant to hide the evidence, and I'm beginning to have second thoughts about her whole story. In short, my friend, I think the whole thing sucks like a Hoover, and we have to empty the bag to get through the dirt."

I took a sip of my coffee, and waited for Kevin to go on.

"The mother is a Sharon Dellaplante, age 20, of Derby. No father is listed on the birth certificate for either child, so I'm not sure there isn't a different guy for each of them. She has been employed for the past 3 years at Our Lady of Perpetual Mercy Church as a sort of secretary and rectory housekeeper. The story I get is that the job came along about the same time as she dropped out of high school, pregnant with her first. Regardless, there was a large life insurance policy, to the tune of $100,000 on each child. To me, that's a bit much for a woman of such, shall we say, modest means."

"Isn't that a lot of life insurance to carry on a kid?" I asked. "I mean I love my babies like nobody knows, but that seems a little extravagant to me."

Kevin explained, "In life insurance, it is possible to get a policy that large on a child. However, the parents have to be carrying a huge policy themselves."

"Define 'huge'," I said.

"$500,000 dollars death benefit."

"Huge it is," I said. "So who pays the bill on that much life insurance, surely not the young Ms. Dellaplante?"

"We're working on that one," said Kevin between bites of his sandwich, "but from all indications it has been paid by Dellaplante Development Corp. Despite the fact that we own the policy, that information gets held in accounting and I have to request a separate file. Don't ask me why, it is what it is. I'll let you know sometime later this week for sure."

"So what do you need from me Kev? It still seems to me, between you and the cops, you've got this one pretty much covered. Not that I would ever turn down work, but what's the plan?"

"Actually, I think the plan is still forming. But where you could be a big help is to talk to Ms. Dellaplante. I've tried getting a hold of her, but no luck. I've also tried getting through to the Cheektowaga PD, Hamburg PD, and the Sheriff's Department with the same kinda luck. I want to know if they have any suspects, or are we looking at mom as the primary. Like I said Joe, there's something wrong here. Too much money involved to have this many unanswered questions. People like you, Joe, they talk to you."

"Yeah," I said, "I'm a likeable guy." We both laughed the nervous laugh of two men who didn't believe a word of what they said. I asked, "So when do I start?"

"As far as I'm concerned, the clock is ticking."

LAKE EFFECT

He agreed to my usual fees plus expenses, and to a retainer. Normally, I wouldn't ask for one from Kevin, but didn't mind asking for one from Kellerman Insurance. Besides, I could use the cash. We finished our lunches, and promised to keep each other informed. It was almost two o'clock in the afternoon, so rather than heading home directly, I opted to take a swing down by the lake to take a look at the scene. I wanted to get home to Paula and the kids but thought it would be more productive to head down and see where everything took place. From the diner, it took me about five minutes to get to the boat launch at Locksley Park. Being winter, there was nobody there. I have to admit that ordinarily it would be just that kind of solitude would bring me an inner peace, but not today. An obtrusive yellow barricade stood vigil around the launch, a grim reminder of a sickening discovery. All I could think about today were those two kids, and how much I really wanted to help find whoever killed them. I stared at the boat launch, trying to imagine what happened in those cold moments. I pictured the way the van went into the water from what Garner told me. I got out of the car to get a better look. The wind off the water was biting cold, and I turned up the collar of my navy pea coat and shoved my hands deep into the pockets to keep warm.

I walked past the barricade and down the launch ramp towards the water, trying to trace the path of the van in my mind. If the mother's story was true, the carjackers would have probably taken the van down the I-90 to Hamburg, and down Camp Road to the lake, along Route 5 to the nearest dumping spot along the lake, the boat launch at Locksley Park. I couldn't figure out why they went to the trouble to back it in, unless they did it because it was front wheel drive and that would push the van deeper and faster into the water. That made a sick sort of sense. I looked out over the lake and noticed that the sun was reflecting off the choppy surface.

I was so absorbed that I didn't hear the footsteps behind me. A tap on my shoulder was enough to snap me out of my concentration. I spun around to see an older guy with a fishing pole, tackle box and bait bag. He looked to be about 45, maybe 50, thin with a receding hairline under his old woolen watch-style cap. He was wearing an old olive green fatigue jacket over a heavy gray hooded sweatshirt, duck boots, and the smoky smell of thousands of Camel cigarettes. "Kinda cold to be standing around down here, don't ya think?"

"Yeah," I replied, "I suppose it is."

"You ain't no fisherman, so what brings you here?"

"Came to look at the water."

"I know what you mean," the man said. "I sometimes come down here to watch her roll. That's why I love to fish. Catching somethin's just icin' on the cake."

It occurred to me this guy might be here enough to have seen what happened, so I took a shot. "My name's Joe," I said, sticking my hand out.

"Mickey," he said, shaking my gloved hand with his.

"You come down here a lot, do ya, buddy?" I asked him.

"Been coming down here for years," he coughed, hacking from years of tobacco and exposure. "Used to like ice fishing, but this no ice on the lake at Christmas is kinda weird. The lake should be at least partially frozen by now. Usually, ice anywhere on the lake gets pushed by the winds and currents down to our end of the lake. Our end is usually the first to have the ice in the winter, and the last to lose it in the spring. When I was younger, it was real common for ice fishermen to drive their cars right to their fishin' spot. Lately, it's been rare to walk on the ice, never mind drive on it."

"You ever see anything down here, something not right, you know what I mean?" I asked.

"You mean like that van they pulled outta here? Damn cruel shame about them kids."

"I know."

"Are you a cop or something, mister?"

"Something like that. Did you see it go in?"

"Naw, man, didn't see nothin' like that. Saw it coming out, but not going in."

"Any of your fishing buddies able to help me?" I asked. I shivered and stamped my feet to stay warm.

LAKE EFFECT

"Maybe Herbie or Casey saw somethin'. They come down here as much as I do."

"Herbie or Casey coming down here today?"

"We didn't have no date or anything, Mister. I just see'em here when I come fishin'."

"Here's my card, pal," I said, handing it to him. "If you're talking to Herbie or Casey, or anybody down here that might have seen anything, give me a call."

"Sure. Hey, you looking to get the guys that did this to them kids? Did you say you were a cop or something?"

"Something. Give me a call if you think of anything, okay."

I went back up the incline to my Jeep Cherokee, started it up and turned towards home. I thought about Kevin, and how he was suspicious of the mother of the Dellaplante kids. Why would he be so convinced she was guilty of killing her kids? It wasn't like Kevin to jump to those kinds of conclusions without having something to go on. Was there something he wasn't telling me about the case? I tried to keep an open mind to everything. It seemed to me that whoever did this, it didn't seem as random as the media made it sound. If it were random, and the carjackers just wanted to dump the van, why in the lake, and why would they go to the extra time and trouble to actually back the van into the water when it would have been easier to just abandon it in the lot. Kevin was right about one thing; things weren't making a lot of sense.

Three

Monday morning found me in my office, figuring out which bill wasn't going to get paid this week. I liked to get to the office, and hopefully out of the office, before my secretary. Samantha Kelly, or Sam as she preferred to be called, ran my office with a scary effectiveness. Sam was a pretty girl, tall at 5'10" with wavy red hair and deep green eyes. She was always dressed professionally, and preferred pants to a skirt or a dress. She had been with me for a while, and we had developed a trust and respect for each other's expertise. The sign on the door said Banks Investigations. But make no mistake about it, Sam was in charge. And so it was when she came into the office that morning.

"Joe? You in back there?" she called back to my office.

"Yup, just going through the priority list. Gonna be out and about most of the day today."

"We have a new case? Or are you going into hiding until next month?"

"We have a case, and the client is Kellerman Life Insurance."

"Great, maybe we'll get paid this time, too?" Sam was incredibly loyal, but even she liked being able to cash a paycheck once in a while.

"Better than average chance this time, Sam. Retainer and everything."

"Good. Bad enough I have to dodge bill collectors for you here, but I'm starting to have to deal with them at home, too. What's the case, Joe?"

"Carjacking and murder of the Dellaplante kids. An old friend over at Kellerman Insurance wants us to dig up what we can before they consider paying the death benefit on the kids."

"So what do you need me to do? Between lies to the bill collectors, that is."

"Okay, Sam, message received and understood. In between dodges, do a favor. Call Kevin Garner at Kellerman Insurance and get the name and address of the people paying the life insurance for Sharon Dellaplante. And while you're at it, give your pal Jeanine at the Cheektowaga PD a ring and see if they have any leads on the guys that stole Ms. Dellaplante's van." This would give me the chance to get down to Derby and talk to Ms. Dellaplante myself. Derby was only 15 or 20 minutes from my office in Hamburg.

"Sure," Sam said. "Anything else?"

"Naw, that ought to do it Sam. Call me if you come up with anything, okay?"

I grabbed my cell phone and headed out the door to the Jeep. A quick look at my watch told me that Kyle and Amanda would both be up and had breakfast, so I gave Paula a call to check in for the morning. "Hi, honey, how's everything this morning?" I asked.

"Pretty good. Are you on the road?"

"Yeah, on my way to Derby. How are the kids?"

Paula started to laugh. "You won't believe what Amanda did this morning. I went upstairs to get them some clothes, and when I got back to the family room, your daughter was running around butt naked. No jammies, no onesie, no diaper, no nothing. So I asked her where her diaper was, and she trotted over to the trash can to show me she put it in there, just like Mommy and Daddy do when they change her."

I laughed with her for a minute. It was these times that made being a dad kinda funny, bordering on hysterical. "You know, Paula, our daughter may have a future as a stripper. I can hook her up with my bartender friend in Fort Erie. I hear the Canadian ballet is looking for dancers," I said sarcastically.

"Of course, that's how she's going to support us in our old age. Be careful going to Derby, hon."

"Love you."

"I know. See you tonight."

I arrived at the home of Sharon Dellaplante at about 9:30 in the morning. She lived in a small, singlewide trailer home, with the plastic sheets on the windows visible from the outside. The plastic shook in the breeze, and didn't look like it was very effective keeping out a draft. There were a few children's toys in the front yard left

LAKE EFFECT

out from the last short bout with warmer weather, and a swing set visible to the side. There were two cars in the driveway, an older Ford Fairlane on four cinderblocks under the carport, and a late model Chevy Cavalier. I climbed the three concrete steps to the front door and rang the bell. A young woman came to the door, wearing an old green terrycloth bathrobe, looking like she hadn't been out of bed yet. Her dark brown hair fell in tangled curls around her shoulders, and dark circles rimmed her bloodshot and angry eyes

"Yes? Can I help you?" she asked, her eyes just slits against the winter sunshine.

"I'm Joe Banks with Banks Investigations. Are you Sharon Dellaplante?"

"No, I'm her sister, Maddy. What do you want?"

The sister was very, very defensive, and very protective. She was less thrilled with the intrusion than I was before I got there. I had to admire her for it. I took out my I.D. and showed it to her. She glared at it, then at me. "I'm a private investigator, and I've been hired to ask a few questions about the deaths of her children, and I figured I would start with Sharon. Will she be available later on this afternoon?"

"I don't know," Maddy shot back, with just a little more venom. "She's at the funeral home, planning the burial of her children. I'm staying with her to help out while she gets through this nightmare. Do you have any idea how long it takes to plan to bury two beautiful babies, Mr. Banks?"

"No, I don't," I sighed.

"Neither do I. So you and your questions will have to start someplace else, like maybe with the scumbags who killed my niece and nephew. Or are you like the police and the rest of them, ready to assume Sharon did this to her own kids?" Her anger was beginning to overflow, and I could see the tears welling up in her eyes. I offered my condolences to a slamming door, and walked back through the cold and the slush to my car. Dellaplante's sister Maddy made me feel about three feet tall, but I had learned a long time ago it wasn't personal, that it was a part of the business. A part I never really

23

cared for.

Once back in the car I called the office to see if Sam had made any progress at all. "Banks Investigations," she answered.

"Hey Sam, it's me."

"Hi boss, what's up?"

"Nothing happening down here. I missed Sharon Dellaplante, and ran face first into her sister. It wasn't pretty. What do you have for me?"

"Jeanine tells me the cops up there don't have much to go on, due to the description they got from a couple of witnesses in the parking lot of two men in black ski masks who, and I'm quoting here, 'sounded like black guys'. There were not a lot of witnesses, which is weird for the Christmas shopping season at the Galleria. There was nothing identifying at the scene that anyone could say was out of place, and they are in a pissing contest with the Hamburg cops and Sheriff's Department as to who has jurisdiction now. Seems everybody wants the publicity. Maybe they've been watching too many episodes of *Unsolved Mysteries*."

"Probably. Isn't that why we got into this job in the first place?"

I heard Sam laugh on the other end of the line. "I don't know about you Joe, but I took this job for the cushy hours, the fat paycheck, and the interesting, glamorous people we get to meet."

"Yeah, yeah, yeah," I shot back. "Anything from Garner?"

"Left a message with his office to call either me here or you on the cell phone."

That usually meant the game of phone tag with Kevin had begun. "Thanks, Sam. I'll be back by about 11:30. I'm gonna make a stop on the way back."

"Make one of those stops for lunch, would ya? I have such a taste for Chinese food today. Must be the weather."

"Okay, Hong Kong Dynasty alright with you?"

"Fine. Just don't forget the hot mustard and fortune cookies this time."

"Alright. See ya in a bit." I turned the Jeep down Route 5 towards Hamburg, figuring I would make a short stop at Our Lady of Perpetual

LAKE EFFECT

Mercy church to talk to Ms. Dellaplante's employer. I was hoping to get any information that might help make sense of what happened to those kids. It only took about fifteen minutes to get to the church, which sat directly across the street from the lake. I imagine divine providence, and good real estate, gave it a spectacular view of the water, with some of the prettiest sunsets anywhere. I walked up to the old oak door of the rectory and rang the bell. It took a minute or two for an older woman to answer the door.

"May I help you, sir?" she asked. She was a thin woman, frail looking in appearance with a long, angular face. Her hair was silvery blonde, her eyes a grayish-blue, with no particular humor in them. Her navy blue wool skirt suit ended modestly past her knees, and the air around her was an odd mix of cedar and Chanel No. 5. It was a scent unique to women in their 60's, and while she didn't necessarily look it, my guess was she hid her age well. She regarded me as an intrusion upon her tight schedule.

I extended my card, and she took it in her slender, well-manicured fingers. She looked over her half-lens glasses at the card, then her eyes met mine. "I'm Joe Banks with Banks Investigations. Could I have a few minutes of your time, please?"

"Please come in, Mr. Banks," she said, scowling. "I am Mrs. Lawrence, the church's secretary."

" I have a few questions to ask regarding Sharon Dellaplante," I said as I walked into the vestibule. It was a small area with tan carpeting and off-white walls. There were the usual donation acknowledgements on the outside wall. "How long has she worked for the parish?"

"Three years, since she dropped out of high school. Her parents insisted she work if she was not going to finish school, and her father and the monsignor are long time friends. The monsignor took her in and gave her a position with the parish."

"So she was working here while she was pregnant with both her children?" I asked.

"Yes, and it was quite a problem for her parents, and for the church. You realize, of course, she never married." Her voice was fairly dripping with self-righteous indignation.

"I understand that. Did she ever speak of the father of the two children?"

"She never did, not to mention a name or anything. She spoke of love, but it was more like lust I suspect, the way two immature adolescents think of love."

"They do get the two confused, don't they. How is Sharon to work with?"

"She is pleasant enough, I suppose. Cheerful most of the time, in fact. Mr. Banks, I may not have approved of her choices or her lifestyle, but that does not mean I don't like her personally."

"You just wouldn't want your son dating her?"

"Actually, Mr. Banks," she said, "My son has dated her."

"I see," I replied, more than just a little surprised. "Are they still seeing each other?"

"No," said Mrs. Lawrence abruptly.

"Is there anything else you can tell me about Miss Dellaplante?"

"Nothing comes to mind Mister, Banks is it? But I do have your card if I think of anything else."

"Thank you for your time Miss, um, Lawrence."

"That's Mrs. Lawrence," she corrected.

"Right," I smiled at her, enjoying it a little bit more than I should. Just another victim of the legendary Joe Banks charm.

I went out to the Jeep, and headed back to the office. On the trip back, I thought about what the Lawrence woman said. Her son dated Sharon Dellaplante, maybe more than casually if I was reading her right. It was obvious she didn't approve of it, but I wondered why. I was beginning to think I should check into her son.

Four

Back at the office, Sam had hot tea and napkins ready for lunch. I set the brown bag holding the Chinese food on the table in our makeshift conference room, and hung up my coat. It had been a long, cold, frustrating morning, and I hoped that a hot lunch would take the edge off and lead to a better afternoon. Sam took her Hunan chicken and egg roll, and her customary packets of hot mustard sauce. I don't know why she eats everything so spicy. It must be a redhead thing. I stuck with my basic beef lo mein, simple and by comparison, bland. Halfway through lunch the phone rang, and I got up to get it.

"Banks Investigations," I answered.

"Joseph Banks?" the man's voice on the other end asked.

"Speaking," I said. "What can I do for you, sir?"

"My name is Frank Dellaplante, and you can start by telling me what the hell you are doing investigating my daughter."

"Mr. Dellaplante, I was hired by Kellerman Insurance to look into the deaths of your grandchildren. Given the amount of cash involved, they felt it important to be sure everything is in proper order."

"What do you mean by 'proper order', Banks? Do you and those Kellerman people think Sharon killed her own kids?" he asked. I hate it when people refer to me by my last name. It makes me think they don't like me.

"What I mean, Mr. Dellaplante, is that the insurance company wants to be cautious regarding the possibility of fraud. That amount of money can be a great temptation to certain people, wouldn't you agree?" I asked, being as polite as I could.

"I am warning you, Banks. If you want to do your little investigations, why not do it trying to find the real killers, and leave the innocent mother of the two victims alone!" He sounded outraged that anyone would ever have anything but reverie for his grandchildren, and for his brave daughter, who was valiantly trying to carry on without her children. I was right, he didn't like me.

"I can appreciate what you're doing Mr. Dellaplante. But in all

27

fairness, I don't tell you how to conduct your business. So you'll understand, I hope, when I tell you I intend to continue with the investigation, regardless of where it ultimately leads. I think your grandchildren deserve nothing less, don't you?" For a moment I thought I could hear his face turn crimson, with that little rush of steam you see in the Saturday cartoons. I chuckled to myself at that thought.

"Mr. Banks, it is abundantly clear to me that you have no idea what you are doing, and with whom you are dealing."

"Mr. Dellaplante, you may be right. But my problem has always been that I never let that stop me. Are we finished, because my lo mein is getting cold."

The other end of the line clicked audibly, almost as if his very certain slamming of the phone could be transmitted electronically to my receiver. I walked back to the conference room and sat down to finish lunch. Sam looked up from her plate, face flushed from the spicy food. "Who was that?" she asked.

"Another Dellaplante family member who wants to join the Joe Banks fan club," I said, slurping a noodle.

"Apparently a Dale Carnegie graduate," Sam said. "You have that kind of influence, bringing out the best in people."

"Sarcasm won't get you anywhere, Sam."

"Just another service I provide, boss," she smiled.

I smiled in acknowledgement, and grabbed another mouthful of lunch. Dellaplante tried to shake me up, but somehow it didn't sound as much like a father attacking a potential foe, as much as a man who was frightened of something. Not of me, as near as I could tell, but frightened none the less. There was obviously something more going on here, and I am sure the Dellaplante family and I had not finished with each other. "Anything else exciting happen this morning?" I asked.

Sam looked off into space for a second, then said, "There was a call from this guy named Mickey Galvin. I've never heard of him, but he said you met at the boat launch in Locksley Park. Ring a bell?"

LAKE EFFECT

"Yeah, it does. Did he leave a number?" I asked.

"No, but he told me he, Herbie and Casey were gonna be out fishing this afternoon if you wanted to talk to them. Kinda cold for fishing, isn't it?" Sam asked. "I mean, I know there's no ice or anything out there, but it's still awfully cold to be standing around waiting for the fish."

"Trust me Sam, for these guys, it's not really about the fish."

"So who are these guys anyway?" Sam asked quizzically.

"Possible witnesses to the Dellaplante case. Gonna slide out there after lunch, I think," I told her. "I spoke to Mickey at the launch late yesterday, and he told me Herbie and Casey, whoever they are, might have seen something."

"Coming back at all this afternoon?"

"I don't know, Sam. I'll check in."

"Are you at least going to finish your egg roll?" I swear I have no idea how she can eat like that and not weigh more than she does. I rolled my eyes, slid the egg roll across to her, and grabbed my coat.

It only took me a few minutes to get to the boat launch. I parked up in the lot, and walked the 200 yards or so down to where the three men were fishing. I could smell the cigarettes at about 50 yards downwind. As I got closer, Mickey looked up, nodded his head in recognition.

"Hey, Joe Banks!" he hollered, as if we were friends all our lives.

"What's up, Mickey," I called back. "I heard you called my office."

"Yeah, yeah, hey, my guys here saw somethin' might help you out. This here's Herbie Gubatosi, and the guy on the end there is Casey Kasparczak. His real name is Casimir, but he really hates that, so we call him Casey. They was here that night they sent the van into the lake."

I walked down the beach a few feet to Herbie, who was just casting out into the lake. Herbie Gubatosi looked like he was in his late 40's or early 50's, with dark brown hair and eyes. He looked younger because he showed no signs of graying. He was probably three days past his last shave, and at least that far past his last shower. Just a

RONALD W. ADAMS

hunch, but I'd have guessed the fish in his creel smelled better.

"I'm Joe Banks," I said, putting my hand out to shake his. He preferred to hang on to his pole and reel. "Mickey tells me you were here the night they put that van in the lake."

"You a cop?" Herbie grunted. "Already told the cops what I know."

"That didn't take too freakin' long," Casey muttered under his breath. Herbie shot him a nasty look, and Casey looked away.

"No, not a cop, I'm a private investigator." I hated the abbreviation P.I., made me think of a bad television show with people in loud shirts and Ferraris.

"So you're a rent-a-cop."

I smiled at the reference. It seemed appropriate. "Alright, I can live with that. Did you see something that night? I got two dead kids and nobody to blame, and I really hate that. If you saw something down here that can help me out, why don't you just tell me? That way, you can get back to fishing, and I can get out of your face. It's a win-win all the way around."

Herbie thought about it, then said, "Yeah, we seen the van. Casey and me were sharin' a quart of Millers in back of the building over there. We heard the engine comin', thought it was the town cops or somethin' so we ducked back around the corner. When we looked back, we saw these guys messing around with the front of the van, one on each side. Then they jumped back, and the thing went flying into the water. We heard the splash, and then saw it go under. It was weird, headlights were still on when it was underwater. Casey figured it was some kinda insurance scam, you know, report it stolen and collect the cash for something better. It didn't seem right to me, but, you know, it ain't none of my business so I don't think nothin' of it. Then Mickey tells me about you askin' a bunch of questions, says there might be some kinda reward, seein's how this a big deal with two kids bein' iced."

"Anything else?," I asked. "Were you able to see their faces or anything?"

"What about a reward, Banks?" he asked.

30

LAKE EFFECT

"Herbie, haven't you heard that virtue was it's own reward? Now what else?"

Herbie looked like he was thinking hard, as if thinking didn't exactly come second nature to him. He gave me the impression of a guy who so completely lived to survive the moment, that the past and future meant nothing to him. "They came up the launch ramp, and we seen them taking their masks off, like they was hot or something. It wasn't that cold out, so I don't know what they were doing wearin' em in the first place. I didn't recognize'em, never seen'em before."

"What did they look like, Herbie?"

"They was white, maybe twenties, both of'em looked like they was jocks or somethin', ya know what I mean? They was laughin' at something, then broke into a dead run to a pick-up by Route 5 up the hill there. It was dark, so I couldn't see their faces so good."

"They were a couple of white kids, you sure about that?"

"Dead nuts positive, pal. I ain't too bright, but I know the difference between black and white."

"Would you know'em again if you saw'em?"

"You mean like a lineup or somethin'?"

"Maybe, probably start with some books first. What do you think?"

"Gonna bring Casey, too. He mighta seen somethin' I missed. That okay?"

"Hey, wouldn't be a party without Casey," I said, joking with him. Herbie's stony leather face cracked a smile. They told me they didn't like or trust the cops, and they were always getting a bad time from them when they were down by the lake. I had to admit, nobody would give these guys the benefit of the doubt about much of anything, and so I offered to go with them, to give them a little backup for their story. Maybe then the police would listen if someone who bathed on a regular basis vouched for them. We agreed to meet at the town police department headquarters to go through the mug shots tomorrow afternoon at 2 o'clock, and that Herbie would make sure Casey was there with him. I started back to my Jeep, waving to

RONALD W. ADAMS

Mickey. We would see what happens tomorrow.

Five

It was five thirty when I got home that night. As I pulled into the garage, I could hear the squeals of a pair of two year olds in the middle of dinner. The second the mudroom door opened I heard Amanda scream, "Dadda home!"

I walked over and kissed her on the forehead, then moved over to Kyle, who was covered in ketchup and French fries. Paula was behind the counter, finishing off our dinner. I walked over to her, gave her a big hug and a kiss. "What's for supper, hon?," I asked.

"Meatloaf," she said. "How does that strike you?"

"Sounds great to me. How were the kids today?"

"It was a good day. Kyle managed to do his drawing on the big paper I taped down for them. Amanda opted for a mural, unfortunately. Check it out."

Sure enough, there it was in colorful red, green, blue and black crayon, an abstract masterpiece covering the bottom fourth of the family room wall. At first I was aggravated, and then I was amused. After all, some of Michelangelo's best works were frescos. Say what you will, the kid had potential. I was learning that parents of toddlers had a perspective all their own.

"Amanda, honey, what did you do on the wall?"

"Draw picture, Dadda," she said as proudly as she could. It was impossible to be upset at her. I surrendered.

"Hi Kyle. How's my little buddy tonight?" I asked, running my fingers through his fine blonde hair. He looked up at me with sparkling blue eyes, smiling his big ketchup faced smile. He threw me a big thumbs up sign with his right hand, squinting his left eye at the same time.

Paula watched as she stirred a pan of vegetables, looking up long enough to ask how my day was. I told her about Mickey, Herbie, and Casey, and about Mr. Dellaplante, and how I generally managed to make friends and influence people all over the Southtowns. "Gee," she said, "all that and its still only Monday. You have a busy week ahead of you."

"That's what keeps me going, babe," I replied. "How long before supper?"

"You've got a little time yet."

"I'm gonna go wrestle with the kids for a while."

"I'll call you when it's ready" Paula replied.

I got the kids out of their high chairs, cleaned up the trays and hands and faces. I laid down on the family room floor, and was immediately covered in two year olds. Kyle and Amanda had a lot of energy, and I was more than happy to help them burn it off. Besides, every , I get with them is so very precious, cleaning the wall could wait until after they went to bed. This was our playtime.

We rolled around on the family room floor for a while before Paula called me to the table. She had eaten with the kids already, but kept me company anyway. Say what you will about those guys on the food channel on television, my wife had a way with meatloaf. Suppertime was followed by bath time, which was a favorite time for the kids. I have never heard of any kids actually lining up at the foot of the stairs just to go take a bath. They love the water, and splashing each other as well as Paula and I. After the bath came pajamas, followed by chocolate milk, brushing teeth, and bedtime. I was very lucky that my job allowed me the flexibility to watch the two of them grow and become little people, instead of seeing it all through pictures Paula took while I was out of town. I knew fathers like that, but I could never be one of them.

With the kids put to bed, Paula and I got to talk like two adults. She asked me again about the Dellaplante case. "Somebody is lying, but I'm not sure who, and I'm not sure why," I said.

"What makes you say that, Joe?" she asked.

"Well, I have two guys who saw the van go in the water, who said that what we are dealing with is two white guys in ski masks. I'm going with them to the town police station to go through mug books. But there's something else. They were telling me they saw the guys put the van in reverse, backing into the water. If they were just grabbing the van for a joy ride, why dump it in the lake? If they knew what they had in the van, that they were carrying two kids,

LAKE EFFECT

why would they risk murder for a carjack?"

Paula looked at me with a questioning look. She didn't like when I started thinking like one of them, one of the bad guys. In fact, she once told me I was too good at it, and it made her nervous. "What are you saying, Joe? Someone intentionally killed those kids, and tried to make it look like it was some black kids doing a joy ride gone bad?"

"That's what it looks like, but there's too many questions and not enough answers at this point. It looks to me like someone paid a couple of kids to get rid of those babies, but I haven't figured out why yet. The money is big, but is it big enough?" I was thinking out loud at this point, not really expecting input from anywhere. It was what I did to get the question from the back of my mind out where I could feel it, work with it, and make sense of it. Sometimes it worked.

"Joe, who would want those babies dead? It's too awful to even think about," Paula said, cupping her hands over her mouth in a vain attempt to recapture her words. She knew it was possible, especially since she knew about the insurance money. But to actually contemplate anyone killing those innocent kids, especially with our two sleeping peacefully upstairs, was something she didn't even want to admit. "You're going to have to go back out to Derby tomorrow, aren't you?"

"Yeah," I said. "I have to talk to the Dellaplante's, especially Sharon, and I am probably going to have to talk to the Lawrence woman."

"Do you think they know more than they've told the police already?" Paula asked.

"I don't know, hon, but I think they do. At least I think Mr. Dellaplante knows more than he is telling."

"The more I know about this case, the less I like it."

"Me, too, Paula."

We sat in the evening dark, quiet except for the sounds of the television. Both of us listened to the sounds on the baby monitors, and to our own thoughts. There was a tension in the air, a tension borne of love of a wife for her husband. I knew, because we had felt

35

it before. It was the silence of questions unasked, and answers unspoken. After 15 years of marriage, we have had our comfortable silences, where we felt just fine not speaking. Those were the easy silences that two people who know each other share from time to time, where words were not needed. This silence was thick, and palpable, and uncomfortable. It followed us into our bedroom, still wordless and nervous, until it finally gave way to sleep.

I woke up in a cold sweat, about 3:30 am, shaking. I had the same nightmare that I've had for the past 10 years. I had worked my way to detective in this small town police department on Cape Cod, which means I was getting paid for investigating loud parties in the summer, and false alarms in the tourist trap shops when the power went out in the winter. It was late October, when my partner at the time, Mike Francis, and I were called out to a silent alarm at a little arts and crafts store. We figured it was either a false alarm, or one of the late season break-ins by a local kid with nothing to do. So we got there, it had to be about 11:00 or 11:30 pm, and noticed a flashlight beam moving around the inside of the place through the plate glass window.

In my dream, I watched as Mike motioned that he would take the back, and I would take the front. He disappeared around the back of the building, and I approached the front door at a steep angle. I tried the door handle, and the door moved slightly, with no resistance. I held my breath as I drew my gun from its shoulder harness. I checked the revolver, and all six rounds were in. I pushed the door open as slowly as I could, trying to avoid the squeaking that these old doors are prone to. When it was open just enough for me to slide inside, I moved quickly into the showroom and stayed as low behind the displays as I could. I could see the outline of the suspect about 20 feet away, probably looking for something he could fence, since the store had been closed for at least a month. I stood up, and made my way quietly towards the person, keeping my gun ready, pointed down.

I was no further than ten feet from him when from behind me I heard a voice shout, "Freeze, Police!" The suspect spun, facing me, and opened fire. His eyes were wide and his face was frozen in a

LAKE EFFECT

scream. I heard the first shot whistle past my ear, and felt the sharp, stabbing slam of the second as it went into and through my left shoulder. I never even got off a shot when the force spun me hard to the left and I crashed into a display of clay pots, and over the platform they were arranged on. I felt the warm blood spread down the inside of my jacket, and my head began to swoon. The guy who shot me came over, and took aim while I was lying there, bleeding. I heard a shot, and watched the gunman drop to his knees, then fall forward. I saw Mike's face looking down at me as I lost consciousness.

I got out of bed, still disoriented, and made my way to the master bathroom. I ran the cold water, and splashed my face a few times. I looked at my left shoulder, at the oval scar just underneath the end of my collarbone, and touched it gently. It still amazed me how much it hurt even ten years after the fact. Out of habit I rolled my arm forward and back. Quietly, I went back into the bedroom, where Paula had rolled over and faced away from my side of the bed. I slipped back under the covers, closed my eyes, and there were no more nightmares.

Six

The next morning I showered, got dressed and grabbed my wool pea coat on the way out the door. A quick stop for a cup of coffee at Tim Horton's, and I headed towards Derby to try to catch Sharon Dellaplante. I wondered what I would say to her, wondered what kind of person I would find when I finally met her. It dawned on me that today was Tuesday, and since she was busy making funeral arrangements yesterday, the wake would probably be today. This tidbit of deduction did not make my job any easier at all. To be sure, I pulled over at a little convenient store to check the obituary notices in the newspaper. I was right. I hate it when that happens.

I got to the driveway of Ms. Dellaplante's home, and beside the one up on cinderblocks, there was only one car in the driveway. I really hoped it was hers as I walked up towards the door. It was cold, and the snow crunched under my shoes as I took the three stairs up to the front door of her trailer. I knocked on the door, and stepped back. It took a couple of minutes before she answered the door, a thin, frail looking waif of a girl dressed in baggy sweats. I must have awakened her, as she looked like the short end of a bad night. I had that sick feeling in my stomach again. "Yeah?" she said, groggily. "Who are you?"

"Are you Sharon Dellaplante?" I asked, already knowing the answer.

"Yeah, I'm Sharon. Who are you?"

"My name is Joe Banks," I said. "Your sister probably told you I was here."

"What do you want Mr. Banks? I have a very busy and very long day today. I'm sure you know," she said, looking wearily at my card.

"Yes, I know, I read the paper this morning, and I really am sorry. I won't take a minute or two, if I can come in. It's kinda cold to be talking out here." She nodded, and stepped back from the door to let me in.

Her trailer was neat, and bright for a house that started life as a beer can. There were pictures of her children, David and Sarah, everywhere in the kitchen. I thought of Kyle and Amanda, just waking up at home. "Can I get you a cup of coffee, Mr. Banks," she offered. "It's instant, but I can whip it up in a minute or so."

I thanked her but declined. "Thanks, but I had a cup on the way. I want to help find out what happened to your children, Ms. Dellaplante. I can't say for sure yet, but I don't think this was a random carjacking. Do you think you can answer a few questions for me?"

We sat across from each other at her small kitchen table, and I noticed the high chairs on either side. There were small toys on the floor under the table, and from where I sat I could see the two bibs neatly folded over the backs of the chairs. There was insurance paperwork on the table, an envelope from the funeral home, and three food stamp booklets. I watched her as she brushed the strands of sandy brown hair from her face, and the sleep from her eyes. She was a very pretty girl, with hazel eyes that had an older look to them, and high cheekbones that gave her face an almost angelic look. She had smaller, more delicate features than her sister Maddy, and something about her made you want to protect her. Her eyes darted back and forth between me, and the two empty highchairs.

"You know, Mr. Banks, I could never get them to sleep past 7 in the morning. They would always wake up early and play in their cribs for a while. I could hear them in my room, and I would just be so tired, and try to sleep a few minutes longer. I thought, as long as they were safe in their cribs, I could get a little bit more sleep," she said as her voice started to crack. "I would get them up, and we would watch Sesame Street before breakfast, and then I would fix them a waffle or French toast, and we would have breakfast together."

She motioned to the highchair to her right. "That was David's chair, and that one over there was Sarah's." Her eyes began to well up, and her voice was shaking. She wiped her eyes with the sleeve of her robe. "You said you had questions for me?"

"If you think you're up to it. I want to know more about what happened at the Galleria parking lot. Think you can tell me, Sharon?"

LAKE EFFECT

I asked.

"I remember it was dark, and I had just put the bags in the back of the van," she started, regaining her composure. "David and Sarah were already in their car seats, and I finished putting the bags away and was going to the driver's side door to get in when these guys jumped me from behind. I couldn't see their faces but they had this street kinda talk going, you know what I mean? They sounded like black guys, the way they talk."

"Anyway, one of them grabbed me, and the other one says 'Dump the bitch, we just want the ride'. So they throw me over a snow bank, jump in the car and take off. I ran after them, as if I could catch up to them. They had my babies in there, I couldn't just let'em go! But it was no use, I couldn't get'em, so I ran back to Sears to call the police."

"Then what happened, Sharon?" I asked, just trying to keep her going.

"They got there maybe 10 or 15 minutes later and took my statement. It all happened so fast, and they were asking so many questions. I couldn't remember what year my van was, what the plate number was, or anything. I was so scared. I was shaking so badly I couldn't even hold a pen. A woman officer talked to me for a while, and I managed to calm down a little. They wrote everything down about the way I told you."

"Can you tell me anything else about the men who jumped you? This could be very important."

Sharon stopped to think for a minute. She took a sip from her coffee cup, and then went on. "Like I said, Mr. Banks, I never really got a good look at'em. Stupid thing though, I remember the guy who grabbed me was wearing the same cologne as this guy I was sort of seein'. What the hell was the name of it? I can't remember it right now."

"Were there just two of them, Sharon? Did you see or hear more than the two guys?"

Sharon shook her head.

"This is very important, Sharon," I said to her. "Is there anybody you can think of that would want to hurt you, or your kids, or your family?"

"You mean, bad enough to want to kill my two babies?" she asked, choking back a sob.

"Yeah, that bad."

"No, I never hurt anyone that bad, that they would, I mean what kind of…" , her voice trailed off, as she started to withdraw at the thought of anything like that. I hated to ask the next question, but I had a feeling that if I didn't, I wouldn't get a second chance.

"Sharon," I started, "why did you carry so much life insurance on yourself and the children?"

She looked as if someone slapped her, hard. "What?!"

"There is a very large life insurance policy on each of the two babies, $100,000 dollars, and a $500,000 policy on you. A lot of people are asking why, and I have to admit, I'm one of them. And the people at Kellerman Life Insurance, the one's who are carrying the policy, want to know, maybe have a right to know, what's going on before they pay out a whole lot of money."

"But, Mr. Banks, I really don't know what you're talking about. I couldn't afford a life insurance policy like that. My father may have this big development company, but I haven't even talked to him since Sarah was born. Apparently, he doesn't approve of the way his grandchildren came into the world. If I had any kind of money at all, do you think I would live in this neighborhood of trailer trash, never mind in a goddamn trailer? I didn't put that kind of life insurance on me or the kids, I don't have any life insurance at all."

"You mean to tell me you are going to get two hundred thousand dollars for the deaths of your two children, and you haven't the foggiest idea why or how or who? Am I expected to believe that?"

"You have to believe me, Mr. Banks. I don't have any idea who put a big life insurance policy on my kids and me. I didn't. Look at me! I mean, do I look I have a lot of disposable income?"

I came ready to accuse her of killing her kids for the insurance money. I felt as if someone broadsided me and took off, leaving me bruised and confused. I was becoming convinced she didn't know

LAKE EFFECT

anything about the money, and didn't know who did. This gave me no satisfaction at all. Usually I knew what the next move was, but this time I was lost. "Ms. Dellaplante, what about the father of your children? Where is he through all of this? I mean, it's obvious to me that your situation is tough, but shouldn't he at least be around somewhere?"

She glared at me intensely. I hit a very raw nerve there, and she practically growled. "That son of a bitch split right after Sarah was born. Told me he found someone better, some rich bitch who would take care of him in style. Said he didn't want to be anywhere near the white trash...." She stopped, choking on her tears.

I stood up, handed her my business card, and said, "Listen, Sharon, I am only interested in taking care of the people who killed your kids. I want to find them and make sure they spend a long time in a small room. If you think of anything, anything at all...."

She took my card, staring at it for a minute. She wiped her eyes with her hands and asked, "Mr. Banks, are you any good at this?"

"I have my days," I said as I headed out the door.

Seven

I got back to the office late in the morning, and almost immediately regretted it. The phone was ringing, and Sam was nowhere to be found. I picked it up on the fourth ring, long enough that we sound too busy to jump on the phone calls, short enough that any potential customers won't hang up. "Banks Investigations," I informed the party calling.

"Is this Mr. Banks?" asked a very angry person on the other end.

"Yeah, this is Joe Banks, what can I do for you?"

"This is Frank Dellaplante again, Banks. I thought we had been all through this, I thought we had agreed that you would keep out of this entire matter. Did I not make myself clear to you? Have you perhaps misunderstood me? Are you that goddamned stupid?" I think he was angry.

"Let me re-cap," I said as calmly as I could, "and you stop me if I go wrong here. You want me to drop my investigation of the deaths of your two grandchildren, and you want me to leave your daughter and any one else she knows out of the investigation, thereby letting sleeping dogs lie. Did I get it right?"

"So we do understand each other, Banks."

"No, I don't think we do, Mr. Dellaplante. If you are finished with your tough guy act, and your toothless threats, and your egomaniacal, self-aggrandizing soliloquy, I'll explain why. I am going to continue to find out what happened, why it happened, who's responsible, and why you're so dead set against my doing just that. So I do understand exactly what you are telling me, I just choose to ignore you. Is there anything else you'd like to tell me, Mr. Dellaplante? Like for instance, why do you not care who killed your daughter's children? Why do you seem to be so insistent about keeping me from doing my job?" I do righteous indignation well, and I hoped I had pissed him off enough to get him to tell me something I could use.

It took a moment for Dellaplante to regain his composure, and I fully expected him to launch into yet another tirade. What he did

45

next surprised me. "If you are bound and determined to follow this to the end, Mr. Banks, then we should meet face to face. Are you available to meet me at Briarwood for lunch today?"

After the initial shock wore off, I remembered I told Mickey and the boys to meet me at the police station to run through mug books at 2 o'clock. "I have a previous engagement at two, but I could meet you at noon."

"Fine, I'll expect you at twelve then. Good day, Mr. Banks." And I heard the sound of a definitive click on the other end of the line.

Sam came in just as I hung up the phone, with two cups of coffee. She set one in front of me, and the other on her side of the desk. "I know I'm late," she said. "Does the coffee help?"

"You think you can waltz in here at any time you want, and bribe me into silence with a mere cup of coffee?" I asked in my most stern voice.

"There's a chocolate chip bagel in the bag, too," she smiled.

"Gimme and I know nothin'." It was a system that worked for us.

I took a sip of the coffee, and a bite of the bagel, and took a deep breath. Life was returning to normal. "Who did I miss on the phone, Joe?" Sam asked.

"Frank Dellaplante, with more words of encouragement for me. But on the plus side I will be lunching at Briarwood Country Club this afternoon."

"Isn't that special," Sam shot back. "Last meal of a condemned man?"

"Miss Samantha, I am surprised at you. Could it just be that we have reached an understanding, and that as two men we wish to get to the root of this heinous crime, and allow his daughter some peace of mind regarding the murder of her children?"

"No," she said matter of factly.

"You're right, but he is beginning to piss me off, and I am fairly certain I have become a major pain in the ass to him. At first he was trying to threaten me again, the next thing I know I'm invited for lunch. I don't get it, but I'm going with it for now. Also, so you

LAKE EFFECT

know, I have been talking with Sharon Dellaplante, and with any luck she'll be calling back sometime this afternoon. I will be at the Hamburg Town Hall with the 'Three Stooges of the Lake' from about two o'clock. Give her the cell number if she calls, okay?"

"Okay, Joe. Hey, you want me to pester Kevin again today?"

"Sure, Sam. Make sure you tell his secretary you're calling in regards to your baby's pending paternity test. That'll get a response."

"I'm sure it will," she laughed.

It was a few minutes before noon when I arrived at the Briarwood Country Club. The winter did nothing to detract from the stately appearance of the grounds. In fact, the crystalline snow made it appear even more picturesque. The club had undergone a bit of a renaissance in recent days. The club was purchased by a major golf course developer, who poured a great deal of cash into the place. It paid off in making the memberships more affordable, so that even average guys like me could afford to be basic level members. Once inside, I took the long way to the club's restaurant, strolling past the member trophies and plaques. I turned left towards the restaurant, and opted to wait for Mr. Dellaplante in the bar. It wasn't going to be a long wait, as I watched Dellaplante make his way through the front door of the restaurant. I had seen his pictures on numerous occasions in the local paper. Every time his company opened a new strip mall, or office complex, or, on the odd occasion, a low income housing project, he was right there to cut the ribbon. I waited until he was seated, and until the bartender brought me my beer, and then made my way to his table.

"Mr. Banks, I presume. Please sit down," Dellaplante said, motioning me to a chair across from him.

"Mr. Dellaplante," I acknowledged. We sat in the icy silence of two adversaries, each sizing up the other. He was not what I expected. Dellaplante was a little older than me, late forties I guessed. He was thin and wiry, and though I couldn't get a read on his height because we were sitting. He didn't strike me as all that tall. His hair was a sandy blonde, and his eyes steel gray and cold, and they were focused. I could tell he was used to being intimidating, and didn't like it at all when he wasn't. The deafening, stagnant silence hung between us for a moment, until I said with a smile, "Thanks for the invitation to lunch. Was there something specific you wanted to talk about, or did I successfully charm you into being my friend?"

Dellaplante glared at me, then offered an icy smile. "You probably do believe yourself charming, Mr. Banks. I, however, appear to be completely immune. No, I have specific issues I need to discuss with you. You see, there may be more to this business involving my daughter then either you or she can know."

I took a sip of my beer; let it sit in my mouth for a moment before swallowing. Instead of playing the sarcastic wise guy, which I have a tendency to do, I opted to take my time with him. He obviously had something to say, and I was determined to let him say it. "Mr. Dellaplante, if it will make you feel any better, I don't believe your daughter had anything to do with the deaths of your two grandchildren."

"Of course she didn't," he replied. "My daughter Sharon may have lived a life I have not been particularly proud of, but she was a completely devoted and loving mother to her babies, and has never even so much as spoken to them harshly, that I can account for. She is most certainly innocent, Mr. Banks."

A young man in a white shirt, back pants with matching black Reeboks and a black cartoon character tie came over to take our order. Dellaplante ordered an open-faced filet mignon sandwich, with a glass of mid-range California merlot. I opted for the club sandwich and another Sam Adams. "Mr. Dellaplante, I believe somebody knew the two kids were in the back of the van, and they meant to kill them. I want to find out who, and I want to find out why. And I will take all the help in that I can get, from whom ever is willing to help me."

His eyes softened when he heard this, but only briefly. "Understand this, Mr. Banks. I find your intrusion into my family's life intolerable. So I have two options. One, I can ignore you, and somehow hope you will go away. Or two, I can help you find what you're after, and you go away faster."

LAKE EFFECT

"Have you decided which way you're leaning?" I asked.

"I'll let you know before lunch is over."

"In that case, I hope you don't mind if I ask you a few questions?"

Dellaplante chuckled as he took the glass of wine from the waiter, who returned with our drinks. "You are persistent."

"I have been accused. Do you know of anyone who would want to deliberately hurt your family like this?"

"A man in my position will sometimes have his detractors. I don't go out of my way to make enemies, but I will admit I have some. But one who would kill two innocent children? Nobody I can think of hates me that much."

"I don't suppose you know anything about a big money insurance policy on your daughter and grandchildren, do you?"

Dellaplante's expression darkened. His face flushed for a moment before the expected denial. "I don't know anything about that," he said. I knew he'd say that. He began to pick up his glass of wine, but his right hand shook so badly he put it down again. A small amount of sweat formed on his forehead. He began to wipe his brow with his napkin, and then brought the napkin to his mouth. Dellaplante may be arrogant, but he was also a bad liar, and I seemed to have caught him in a whopper.

"Are you alright, Mr. Dellaplante?" I asked.

"Excuse me, I need to use the restroom," he said, now sweating visibly.

Dellaplante got up from the table, and walked right into the men's room. It took him a few moments, but he returned to the table a little paler than when he left. He started to sip at his wine again, but it became a long swallow as he drained the glass without a breath. "My apologies, Joe. May I call you Joe?" he asked.

"Sure. What was that all about?"

"Been fighting the flu, I guess. It's going around my office, probably picked it up from one of my secretaries, or their kids, or something." It was a weak lie, but I decided not to press him on it. Besides, it was just then that lunch arrived. He motioned for the waitress for another glass of wine.

49

I took a bite of my sandwich and poured my beer into a glass. Ordinarily, I would drink from the bottle, but etiquette overruled my baser instincts. I took a slow drink from my glass, and watched Dellaplante nervously pick at his lunch. That last question rattled him badly, and he was having trouble regaining control.

"A few years ago, Joe," he began, "Dellaplante Development was still evolving from the small construction company that started it. Sharon was still in high school, and her mother was running my office for me while I was hustling for projects. We were very involved with the church; Sharon did readings on Sunday and my wife taught Sunday school for first and second graders. In fact, it was the parish that gave Dellaplante Development our first big job, a complete renovation of the church, rectory and parking lot."

I listened carefully, anxious to hear what he had to say. He took a deep breath, and continued. "There was a woman who worked there at the church office, a Mrs. Lawrence. She had a son, Michael, who was a little older than Sharon. They were involved in a lot of the same activities outside of school, and they became very friendly. Michael Lawrence was a charmer, with a smooth tongue and a persuasive manner. He seemed to be a good boy, from a good home, and he even asked my permission to date Sharon. Nobody does that anymore, nobody. Anyway, he had me snowed, and I gave him a job with the company, and gave him permission to date my daughter."

He took another, longer pause. I managed my best been there, heard that attitude as I took another bite of my sandwich. He picked up his wine glass, and unceremoniously drained it for a second time, then continued with his story. "Anyway, Michael was welcomed as my own son, and had full access to me, my family, and my company. That was my mistake, the son of a bitch. He is a smart kid, very smart, and began to notice some, I guess you could say, unorthodox expenses on some of our bigger projects. Everybody pads things a little, Joe, everybody in construction budgets for little unexpected problems."

I took another drink from my glass. "And do those unexpected problems sometimes include, hmmmm, let's say entertainment

LAKE EFFECT

expenses?" I asked.

His face reddened. "Sarcasm couched in discretionary language. I appreciate that. Yes, let's say entertainment. You have to understand, I am a pillar in this community, and this sort of thing could hurt a number of people. Hell, I was even able to get Sharon a part-time job with the church because of my connections with the archbishop. So you see, discretion is critical. Too many people are involved, too many people are depending on me."

I couldn't resist. "But not so important that you couldn't be blackmailed, or is that what made you such a wonderful target? Because you are so 'important' to so many people?" I asked.

His head bowed, and for a moment he had a look on his face somewhere between remorse and regret. "Yes," he sighed. "When he found out about my, what did you call them, entertainment expenses? Anyway, when he found out about my entertainment expenses, he decided that it would be less expensive to keep him quiet about it to the inspectors and the clients, as well as to my family. Are you familiar with the phrase every man has his price? I learned his price."

"And his price was my life, and everyone and everything in it," he said wearily.

His sob story finally got my attention.

51

Eight

Michael Lawrence was a tall, good-looking kid. I suppose most women would describe him as a hunk, with his blonde haired, hazel-eyed baby face looks. He was smart, charming, well dressed and well mannered. So when he came to Dellaplante Development, straight out of business school, he was a very impressive candidate for the project estimator job. Lawrence was qualified, and proved his worth by bringing in projects for Dellaplante at almost twice the rate as the previous estimator. He was Dellaplante's new golden boy, and was learning how to use his new role to his best advantage.

It was mid-June when he noticed that the estimates he prepared were being altered prior to submission. At first it seemed that the profit margin was being played with, and that was okay with Lawrence. After all, he figured it was Frank Dellaplante's company, and he could do whatever he wanted. But then the changes became bigger and more consistent, and that worried him. It was beginning to look to him like somebody high up wasn't letting him do his job. So after work one night, Lawrence decided he would find out who was trying to screw him and why.

He sat in the accounting office in Dellaplante headquarters, going over the expense reports for the last few projects. Everything itemized, all expenses accounted for, and nothing appeared to be out of place. Then he found it. Under the heading of marketing expenses on the last project was a $2,000.00 payment to NPA Productions of Buffalo. Lawrence worked his way backwards again through office buildings, strip malls, and suburban land development projects and NPA Productions kept popping up. Why, he asked himself, would we be paying a marketing firm for business we already have? The only person in the company with the power to amend or override any of his bids was old man Dellaplante himself. So what was he doing screwing around with the bids?

Lawrence decided to look into NPA Productions. There was no local listing for it, so he decided to check it out on the Internet. There he found a listing for NPA Productions on Grand Cayman

Island, a gambling web site featuring online casino gaming, sports betting, and anything else you can lay odds on. So that's why the old man was jacking the bids up higher, he thought. So he kept looking, and found that despite winning the majority of bids over the past six months, the company was losing big money. In fact, if his MBA taught him anything at all, he reckoned that Dellaplante Development was on the brink of bankruptcy.

Lawrence got to work, making copies of the records, and planning his next moves.

Nine

Dellaplante finished telling me about Michael Lawrence, and I glanced down at my watch. It was nearly two o'clock, and I had promised to meet Herbie and Casey at the Hamburg Police station. I thanked my host for lunch and left him with the customary business card. It was five after two when I fired up the Jeep and headed to the station. I really hate being late, especially with these guys.

When I got there, Herbie and Casey were sitting on a dirty snow bank in front of the station, smoking their generic cigarettes and looking like somebody stole their bicycle. Mickey was pacing back and forth behind them, kicking the snow bank angrily and repeatedly taking my name in vain. I parked my car and got out to meet them. It was 2:20pm, and the fact that I was wearing a suit and tie was not lost on them.

"About goddamn time, Banks. You said you was gonna be here at two o'clock, man. We was here, even got here early. What, you been hangin' out having a leisurely lunch with the suits, man?" Herbie was definitely pissed off. Casey just sat in the snow, puffing on his cigarette and slowly rocking.

"What happened?" I asked Herbie, quite possibly the brains of the outfit. "Did you guys go in, check out the mug books?"

"Yeah, we went in, but they told us to get out when we told'em what we was there for. Said we was full of shit, and probably full of booze. But we weren't, were we Casey?"

Casey just shook his head. "Real assholes," Casey said.

"So they didn't believe you?" I snapped back. "What a surprise, especially given your sophisticated air. That's okay, because I'm getting the impression the guys we really need to find won't be in any mug books. If you want, we'll go back in and take a look."

"M-m-maybe we should guys, ya know, see what they got?" Casey stammered.

They agreed, and the four of us walked back into the police station. The desk sergeant called the investigating officer, a Detective Harry McCleary, who looked us over and shook his head. I shrugged my shoulders, and handed him my card.

"I heard of you, Banks," he said in the friendliest tone he could muster. "What are you doin' with these guys, and what're you doin' messin' with my case?"

"These gentlemen are frequent users of the boat landing, and may be witnesses to the murder of Sarah and David Dellaplante. I'm here to help them take every opportunity to perform their civic duty as citizens of this fine community." I thought that was fairly eloquent. After all, I had just had lunch at a country club.

"The only thing these wino's coulda seen was a hallucination, Banks. C'mon, quit wastin' my time with this", he said, turning his back on us. He took one step to leave and I reached out to tap him on the shoulder.

It was obvious to me McCleary was not going to respond to charm, grace, and decorum. "Listen, asshole, you got somethin' better, we're gone. You don't, what's the big deal? No sweat off you if they look at the mug books, is there?"

He looked at them, and then back at me. I stood about 4 inches taller than McCleary and was at least 50 pounds lighter. Not that I would be stupid enough to do anything physical to him in the station, or anywhere else, but he figured we had a stalemate. "Hmm," he grunted, "take the Bowery Boys down to room three. I'll meet you there."

We went into the room, followed shortly by McCleary and a stack of books. He dropped them abruptly, and told me to call him if we found anything. After an hour and a half, we didn't. They looked upset, like they wanted to be the heroes for a change, only to be cheated again. I talked to them as we left, trying to explain that sometimes the bad guys don't get their pictures taken, and that this was just a long shot anyway. It didn't help.

"What do you mean, Banks? This was just a waste of time? I thought we was gonna help you nail the sicko who offed those poor kids?" Herbie asked me, with genuine hurt on his face.

"Believe me, Herbie, you, Mickey, and Casey have already helped me a lot," I explained. "Just because the cops can't get past the

LAKE EFFECT

grunge look, that's their loss. You keep me posted, day or night, and I'll be there."

"Yeah, but you gonna be on time next time?" Mickey asked.

I nodded, and then offered them a lift. They declined, and said they were going to hit the supermarket for a quart of Miller's before they went home. I climbed in the Jeep and headed back toward the office.

When I got there, Sam handed me a small pile of messages. One was from the electric company for the office, wanting payment. The next was the gas company for the office, similar request. The next was from Kevin Garner, looking for an update. I looked through the mail and prioritized my phone calls, with Kevin winning the number one slot. I quickly dialed his number, and waded through the automated introductory choices before finally getting his extension.

"Investigations, Garner," the voice on the other end answered curtly.

"Kevin, it's Joe Banks. I'm returning your call," I replied.

"Yeah, Joe, how ya doin'? Whaddya got for me, anything?"

"You know the usual, a few suspects, a few threats, making friends and influencing people everywhere I go."

"The bottom line, Joe?"

"I got nothing so far, Kevin, but you'll be happy to know I am making good time getting it."

"Funny, very funny. But if you don't have something one way or the other, I am going to have to authorize payment to the Dellaplante woman whether she deserves it or not. I know this stuff takes time, but I got pressure on me to settle this thing quickly. Do you have anything at all?"

"Okay Kevin, this is what I do have so far. I have a pissed off sister who thinks we are trying to screw her family. I have a couple of winos from the lakeshore that tell me they saw two guys dump the van in the lake. I have a genuinely distraught mother of two dead kids who is too damn naïve to know what the hell is going on, never mind what the deaths of her kids can mean to her financially. And I got one irate son of a bitch in Frank Dellaplante who wants me to check out this guy who works for him, thinking he may be connected 'cause he has something on Dellaplante. Heard anything you can use yet, bud?"

There was a silence on the other end of the line. "By the way," I added, "what do you have for me, man? I could use a little help from you, like who was footing the bill for life insurance that big?"

"Uh, yeah, you did ask me for that," Kevin stammered, the sound of shuffling papers in the near background. "Seems the policies have been paid a year at a time by Dellaplante Development. Make sense to you?"

"Not yet, but I'll keep it in mind in case it does later. I'm just trying to get information, I'll sort it out later."

"Just keep me posted, Joe."

"I always do, Kev. By the way, is there any way you could cut me a check for services so far. A couple of days pay would help keep the wolves from the door."

"Sure. I'll get it out in the mail in the morning."

"I'll drop by your office about nine," I told him.

"You don't trust me, after all these years?"

I laughed. "I trust you, Kevin, it's the post office that makes me suspicious. I'll bring the doughnuts."

We hung up, and I decided the electric and gas companies could wait until I had something good to tell them. Sam must have heard me hang up the phone, because she stuck her head around the corner as soon as I finished. "Up for coffee this afternoon, boss?" she asked with a hopeful smile.

"Sure. I suppose I'll buy, right?" I joked.

"Hey, I'm not the one who went out to a fancy lunch with the richest guy in western New York," Sam shot back, grinning.

"Jealousy is such an ugly thing, Sam. Double cream and double sugar, please."

"You got it, boss. Oh yeah, Paula called. She wants you to pick some things up for dinner tonight. The list is on my desk. Be back in a couple of minutes."

I heard the door shut behind her as she left for the coffee. And it

LAKE EFFECT

never fails, when the secretary leaves, the phone started ringing.

"Banks Investigations," I said into the phone as professionally as possible.

"Mr. Banks?" the female voice on the other end asked. I assumed it was another detective, with deductive reasoning like that.

"Yes, this is Joe Banks. What can I do for you?"

"Mr. Banks, this is Mrs. Barnes, the ER nurse at Mercy Hospital. Do you know a man by the name of Casimir Kasparczak?"

"Yes," I said nervously. "What's wrong?"

"He was brought in here this afternoon, about 30 minutes ago, and we had a hell of a time identifying him. All he had on him was a torn up wallet with one of your business cards in it. If it weren't for his friend who brought him in, we wouldn't even know who he was. His friend insisted we call you. Are you a member of Mr. Kasparczak's family?

"No, I'm not," I said, "but he and his friends were helping me with a case. What happened to him?"

"Judging from the looks of him, and from what the chart says, somebody worked him over really good." She began to read. "Broken eye socket, broken cheekbone, broken ribs, bruises and cuts and abrasions all over the place. I would say he was lucky to still be breathing from the beating he took."

"Is his friend still with him? Kind of a rough looking character, probably wearing a fatigue jacket and sweatshirt?"

"Yes, he is in the room with him now. He wouldn't leave his side the whole time. Funny thing, the two of them don't look like much, but they look like they are all they have in the world."

"Tell his friend to sit tight, I'll be there in a few minutes. Thanks for calling me." I hung up the phone, and thought about Paula and the kids. I called and told her what happened, and that I would be late for supper.

It only took me about 20 minutes to get to Mercy Hospital, in the heart of South Buffalo. There was a light snow falling, gently covering the cars and sidewalks. I pulled into the ER parking area, and went in to see Casey and Mickey. The receptionist told me they

59

had moved him up to the fifth floor, so I headed to the elevator. As soon as I turned the corner out of the elevator I saw Mickey standing outside the room, his head bowed and his hands covering his face. I walked up to him and put my hand on his shoulder. He looked up at me, looking like a man with more questions than answers.

"The nurse told me you was comin', Joe. It happened not fifteen minutes after you left, Casey and me was walkin' past the convenient store on Main Street. Herbie left, he went back down South Park towards the lake. Some sonovabitch hit me on the back of the head with a bat, put me down hard. Then he started hittin' Casey, hard and fast like he meant to kill him, ya know? And, get this, he was laughin' at us, sayin' how we shoulda stayed under the rocks we crawled outta, that kinda shit." I could feel him start to tremble. I put my hand on his shoulder. I didn't want to press him too hard, but I needed to know more about what happened.

"I tried to get up, ya know, tryin' to help Casey, but I got so dizzy, it was hard to stand up. I tried to grab the guy's sleeve, I wound up rippin' it. He was wearing one of those new style Sabres jackets, you know the black one with the emblem on the chest. Anyway, he just stops, and takes off running. The manager at the store said he saw what happened and he called an ambulance. Casey looked like shit, his face and his chest were all bruised, and bleedin'. I thought he was gonna die right there in the ambulance.

"Do you know who it was?" I asked him.

He nodded. "He was one of the guys we saw at the landing that night gettin' outta the van."

"I thought you said they didn't see you?"

"I didn't think they did, Joe. We was in the shadows, they didn't look at us or nothin'. I don't know how he found us." He let out a sad chuckle. "This is the way it always goes. We try to do the right thing and we get screwed. And this time, Casey..." He trailed off, looking down again.

"Did you call the cops?"

"After what happened to Casey this afternoon, I figured it was better comin' to you. You don't treat us like crap, man. Not like

LAKE EFFECT

they do."

"That's okay, Mickey. How is he doing in there?"

"He got beat pretty bad, man. He got beat really bad. Docs are keepin' him out now, lettin' him rest and heal up."

I walked past Mickey and into the room. Casey was lying in the bed, tubes in his arms, wires coming from under his blue hospital gown. The only light came from a fluorescent bulb over the head of the bed, but it only served to make the whole scene starker, more severe. There were the sounds of monitors and beeping alarms to break the silence, and I walked up to the side of the bed. Under the best of conditions, Casey looked like he'd blow away in a strong wind. Lying there in the hospital bed, he looked even more fragile and broken. His face was covered in bruises, his eyes swollen shut.

"What are you gonna do, Mick?" I asked as I walked back out to the hallway.

"Gonna sit here and wait for him. Nurses have been nice, they said I could get something to eat, and said the chairs are pretty comfortable for sleepin'. I got nothin' else to do, man."

"You get checked out? Your head is okay?" I asked him.

"I got a headache, but I'll live. I'm more worried about Casey right now."

"You worry about him, I'll worry about the guy who did this to you two."

I turned to leave, and Mickey grabbed my arm. "Thanks, Joe. Most don't give a damn about what happens to guys like us. Why do you?"

"Because I'm not like most people," I said.

"What are you gonna do now?" Mickey asked.

"Go home for supper," I told him.

Ten

After supper, Paula and I cleaned up the dishes while the kids played in the family room. Kyle and Amanda ran screaming through the family room, the kitchen, the dining room, and the living room, and back. "Gonna catch you, Manda!" Kyle was yelling as he ran after his much faster sister. Amanda was light on her feet, and made a nimble little turn off the throw rug on the linoleum floor in the kitchen. Kyle, who will probably never be as graceful as his sister, tried to adjust to his sister's sudden change of direction and wound up slipping and sliding onto his little diapered butt.

The two of them were tearing around the house when the phone rang. Paula put down the dishtowel and answered it. "Hello?"

"Mrs. Banks, I presume?" the voice on the other end of the line said.

"Yes, who's calling, please?"

"Frank Dellaplante, Mrs. Banks. I would like to speak to your husband, if I may."

"May I ask what this is in regards to?"

"He and I have some business to discuss. May I please speak to him?"

I looked at Paula, giving her the who's-on-the–phone look. She silently mouthed the name, and I motioned for the handset. "Just a minute," she said pleasantly. As she handed me the phone, she mouthed a phrase that was a better description of Dellaplante. I had to struggle not to laugh as I took the phone from her.

"This is Banks," I said, suddenly switching from daddy mode to detective mode.

"Frank Dellaplante here. We need to meet," he said with a sense of urgency.

"Why? What's the problem?"

"It's Michael Lawrence. When and where can we meet?"

"Circle Diner in 2 hours. You know the place?"

"Yes I do, it's that greasy spoon over near the Ford Plant. Why two hours?"

"I have business to finish here, then I'll be able to meet with you. See you in two hours."

I handed the phone back to Paula. "He wants to meet you?" she asked.

I nodded. "Something to do with an employee of his, he thinks the guy might be involved in his grandchildren's murder."

"What do you think?" she asked, handing me another plate.

"I don't know what to think. I told you about Casey, the guy from the landing, getting the living hell beat out of him today?"

"No, you conveniently left that part out. What happened?"

"I don't know, but he looks like somebody might have made an example of him. Got the lake rats all worked up, and I doubt I'll get anything else from them that will be much help."

"Speaking of help, we have two kids who need to get bathed and put in pajamas, so how about helping me?"

"Absolutely," I replied, scooping up Kyle as he tried to run by me. He giggled and squirmed in my arms as I carried him upstairs to the bathroom.

Two hours later I was sitting at the Circle Diner, sipping coffee across the table from a visibly shaken Frank Dellaplante. He was wearing a Harris Tweed jacket, khaki pants, and a black long sleeved polo shirt. His face was drawn, and his hands were clenched hard around his mug of coffee, knuckles blanched nearly as white as the porcelain cup he was holding. I took a sip of mine, and waited for him to say what he had to say. He cleared his throat, as if to begin, then stopped before he said anything. His expression told me he was carefully considering every word.

"You know, Banks, I am a man of some bearing and influence," he began, straining to control his voice. "This makes it even more difficult to ask, so I suppose I will just get right to it. I want to hire you to look into this problem I am having with Michael Lawrence."

I took a slow sip of my coffee, relishing his sudden change in demeanor. This was obviously weighing heavily on him, and the stress of it was showing. "Frank, I have to tell you that I am already working on the case involving your two grandchildren, and you have

LAKE EFFECT

given me a lead on Lawrence already. If the insurance company is already footing the bill, why do you want to pay me to do the same thing?"

"Because, they are only concerned about this from the standpoint of their own loss. I am more concerned about the effects on my family." I was starting to get a sense of what was important to him. Family seemed important, but more from the standpoint of a possession, something he had rather than something he was a part of.

"If you hire me, you should know up front that I would do whatever it is you need me to do, but my way. I will act as I see fit, ask questions to whoever I see fit and relevant, and if my questions become embarrassing or annoying, that's too damn bad. I am an independent private investigator, with the emphasis on independent. I go where the evidence sends me, regardless of where I may wind up."

"Understood and agreed. If this Lawrence had anything to do with the deaths of my grandchildren, I want him caught and I want him punished." I watched his right hand shake as he held his coffee cup to his lips. He struck me as being the type of man who needed desperately to be in control, and who was watching his world slowly spin away from him. His eyes started to fill as I watched him, and then he took a long deep drink to regain his composure. "Do we have a deal, or have I misjudged you again?"

There was that arrogance, though this time with a much thinner veneer. I studied his face, which was more ashen than the last time I saw him. His eyes were cold, passionless, as if his life was draining slowly. I decided I liked him better pissed off. Pleading for help did not suit him well at all. "We have a deal," I said, "and I'm used to being misjudged. Tell me why you think Lawrence had anything to do with the deaths of your grandchildren."

"He hates me, it's a pure and simple motive. He knows that, while I don't approve of their out of wedlock origins, I love my grandchildren. The fastest way to destroy me is to destroy my family, and he will stop at nothing to destroy me!" Dellaplante became instantly aware he was raising his voice. "Nothing!" he hissed.

"You have to admit it, you are not the most likeable individual. In fact, I have a lot of trouble picturing you in the lóving grandfather role. But it is worth it to look into what you've told me, especially for your daughter's children." I told him my fee, and we had an agreement.

"How do you plan to proceed, Mr. Banks?" Dellaplante asked.

"Let's start by explaining to me why your company took out such large life insurance policies on your daughter and grandchildren."

"That's right," he said, smiling weakly. "You are still working for Kellerman Insurance. Tell me, how is my old friend Kevin Garner doing these days?"

"Frank, you're dodging the question. That's beneath you, really. Tell me why the large policies?" I asked him, smiling back.

I could tell by the look on his face he didn't like being called on his name drop. He liked it less that someone he now considered his employee was calling him on it. I watched him closely as he measured his response.

Finally, he said, "The idea of life insurance is to provide for the survivor in the event of an untimely death. I viewed the policies as protecting the family's most valuable asset."

"That's a lot of protection, don't you think?"

"What are your children and wife worth to you, Banks?"

"I suppose you have a point. But I have a question that's beginning to bother me. Should anything happen to Sharon, God forbid, who is the beneficiary?

"Just what are you implying, Banks?" he asked, his face flushing.

"It's a question that's going to need an answer," I told him matter-of-factly.

"I am," he muttered. "I suppose that makes me a prime suspect in your eyes, doesn't it?"

"Beats me, I'm just making all this up as I go along." All those years of Dale Carnegie courses were paying off, I could tell. I watched as Dellaplante turned to leave. He looked back towards me, and shook his head. It was getting late, and I had work to do in the

LAKE EFFECT

morning. I finished my coffee, and looked down at the table and saw the check, still unpaid. Some great detective I am.

Eleven

I left the house before Paula and the kids were up. I wanted to get to Dellaplante Development early enough to catch the now infamous Michael Lawrence in his office. I didn't have an appointment, and I doubted very much he would give me one on such short notice. There is an old Navy saying that it is better to ask forgiveness than permission. I figured that would be my approach. It was a dark, wet, cloudy morning, with a mix of snow and sleet falling steadily. It was just another day in paradise.

The offices and equipment yard of Dellaplante Development was located on Route 20 & 78 near the Route 400 expressway. There was an eight-foot high chain link fence that surrounded the property, with an assortment of construction vehicles of every size and description from large Komatsu cranes to big yellow road graders. The unique whistling sounds of diesel engines starting could be heard everywhere in the yard. The air was thick with diesel fumes as some of the heavier pieces were warming up before going to the job sites. The Jeep slid a little making the turn before hitting a patch of sand and regaining traction. It splashed through the sloppy, half frozen mud in the yard as I pulled into an empty spot besides the one story block building housing the project managers, engineers, and dispatcher's offices. I was glad I had my jeans and Wolverine boots on, and with my wool coat I looked more like a laborer looking for a job than a P.I. That worked for me.

I turned up my coat collar and walked into the building, where I was met by a way to cheerful young brunette receptionist just inside the door. She was dressed in a bulky knit sweater, flannel shirt, and jeans. Her face was bright; her eyes surprisingly deep blue and clear for this early in the morning. "Good morning, sir. Can I help you?" she chirped.

I smiled back. "Yeah, I'm here to see a Michael Lawrence. Is he in this morning?"

"Let me check," she replied, looking down at a schedule book. "Wait a minute, I know, it's right here. He's out for the day today, at a funeral down in Derby, I think. Somebody in Mr. Dellaplante's family, I guess. He's doing the political thing I bet, but that's Mikey. Always playing up to the boss, you know what I mean?"

"Yeah, I've seen my share of office politicians. Never heard that about Lawrence, though." I was trying to keep her talking. It was a crappy day to be out on the road, and if he wasn't here, at least I was going to find out all I could. "I didn't think he and the boss got along at all. Why would he want to go to a funeral for a guy he doesn't even like?"

"It's not Mr. Dellaplante's funeral, silly," she giggled. Her hair framed her face with loose curls, still slightly wet from washing. "Someone in his family, kids or grandkids, something like that. It's real sad. Mikey must be going just so he can score points. They haven't exactly been getting along lately."

"No?" I asked, leaning on the counter.

"Not at all, something about there being problems with expense reports, budget overruns, you know, like money stuff."

"No kidding. Do you know who was screwing them up? I mean, you know what goes on around here. Every good office manager knows everything, don't they?"

She was actually blushing. "Well, Dellaplante hired Mikey to watch the money, keep the costs down, which he was doing. Then all of a sudden the old man was overriding all of Mikey's work, ya know. Like, he didn't want him to do his job anymore. It was real weird, 'cause it wasn't like he was correcting all his work, just the expenses that Dellaplante was submitting. I figure, you know, he's the boss, and it's his company, so whatever."

As much as I hated to end the brilliant Buckleyesque conversation I was having with someone half my age, I thanked her for the information and left. I called the hospital and checked on Casey, and the nurse told me his condition was serious but stable. Visiting hours started at 11 o'clock, so I had plenty of time to get to Kevin Garner's office. Knowing Kevin as I did, I made a mandatory stop at Horton's Donuts for a dozen doughnuts and a couple of cups of coffee.

LAKE EFFECT

I got to his office at about 8:30, and finished my coffee in the Jeep. He arrived in his silver BMW 325i fifteen minutes later. The insurance business had been good to Kevin it seemed. I got out of my car and walked over and greeted him at his. We walked into the building, and into his office together. I put the doughnuts down on his desk, and took out a plain one for myself. Kevin took off his coat and grabbed a chocolate angel crème and the coffee. I sat, coat still on and legs stretched out, while Kevin sat behind his desk. "You really don't trust the mail, do you?" Kevin laughed.

"Hell, Kev, just to be sure I'd get paid, I brought you doughnuts. Does this sound like a man taking chances?" I joked.

He was still laughing when he picked up the phone and punched the intercom. "Lisa, bring in Mr. Banks' check please. Thank you." He hung up the handset. "Done. Now, what have you found out so far?"

I shifted in my chair and filled him in. "What I found out so far is that my instincts tell me the mother is clean, no doubts. There is a guy in the hospital that was helping me out until someone decided to beat the hell out of him. Now it's getting interesting, because Frank Dellaplante has asked me to investigate this case as well, because he suspects a possibly disgruntled employee. I am still operating in fact finding mode, but I am starting to get some opinions."

Kevin's secretary Lisa walked in and handed me an envelope. Lisa was a pleasant distraction, especially because of the money in that envelope. She smiled at me, and I smiled back and thanked her. Kevin broke in and asked, "Would any of those opinions keep me from having to write a really big check?"

"Sadly not. This has nothing to do with the mother, that much I am sure about. What are the cops coming up with, anything we can use?"

"They're treating it as a homicide of course, but right now they still think the mother is involved somehow. She hasn't been really cooperative, and hasn't given up the name of the kids' father yet so they can talk to him. The whole Dellaplante family has been evasive from what they tell me. From what I gather, they are still looking for the black youths Sharon Dellaplante says stole her car. Tell me about the disgruntled employee theory."

I folded the envelope into my inside coat pocket, and took the last bite of my doughnut. After I swallowed, I said, "After talking to Frank Dellaplante, he told me about Michael Lawrence, and how he suspects him because the two of them were close but now have a severe strain on their relationship."

"Does Dellaplante think this guy Lawrence hates him enough to kill?" Kevin asked.

"Believes it enough to pay me to find out."

We each grabbed another doughnut, and chatted a while longer about families, enough to make it friendly and business-like at the same time. "It bothers me that the family is hiding something about those two kids," Kevin said between bites. "And it bothers me that the patriarch of this little family is paying you to look into something potentially separate but related. Sounds to me like more hiding."

I nodded. "Maybe," I said. "But what's being hidden, what does it have to do with those two kids?"

"Isn't that what you're getting paid for, to find out?" Kevin asked.

"Not me, man. I is just the donut delivery guy," I joked, taking a bite of a plain doughnut.

"Yeah, well, that's a hell of a tip in your pocket."

"Did I forget to say thank you?"

"As a matter of fact…" he began.

"Thank you, Kevin," I told him, smiling.

"You're welcome, but to tell you the truth, I didn't do it for you. I did it for your beautiful wife, your lovely children, and of course the gorgeous Samantha."

"Kevin!" I exclaimed, "You, a happily married man with crumb crunchers of your own, have the hots for my innocent little Sam?"

"What? I'm not allowed a fantasy girl? So what if she's not a Hollywood super-model type. I still think she's sexy."

"What would Amy say?"

"Hey, I don't say anything when she ogles the bag boy at the supermarket."

72

LAKE EFFECT

He had a point. Paula had the same reaction to Pierce Brosnan.

"Permit me this one little midlife crisis, will ya, Jiminy Cricket?" he begged. "Besides, I'm harmless."

"Unless of course she's a bacon double cheeseburger."

"Go find out if I have to have the company write another big check, will ya?" Kevin said with a scowl. "And soon. The Dellaplante family is pressing me for a quick settlement."

Grabbing my coat, I said, "I'll keep you posted, Kevin."

I stopped off at the bank on the way to the office, depositing the check and doing the mental gymnastics necessary to figure out what would be left after payroll and after some of the wolves got paid. I made one more stop to pick up bagels for Sam, since I was celebrating the ability to pay her for a change, and made my way to the office.

Twenty minutes later, I pulled in and skated across the icy parking lot to the office. Sam was there, and already had a pot of coffee going. I could see what got Kevin so excited. She was an attractive woman, single, and her self-confidence made her even more attractive. If I wasn't already deeply committed to my own beautiful wife, and my kids, I would be tempted. I pitched the bag of bagels to her, which she caught on the bounce off the desktop. She opened the bag and smiled. "What, no cream cheese?" she asked.

"Sam, we don't even have a toaster in the office," I replied. I handed her an envelope with a paycheck in it.

"Somebody's had a very productive morning. Should I wait to cash it?" Sam asked, reviewing the check.

"Nope. Zero rubber content. Got a partial payment from Kellerman, so we be in bidness. And to make life a little sweeter, we have another client."

Sam raised her eyebrows. "Wow, you have had a busy morning. Who's the second case? O.J. looking for the real killer, I suppose?"

"Close, actually. Frank Dellaplante wants me to look into one of his employees, a Michael Lawrence. He thinks Lawrence had the kids killed to get to him. So he wants me to find out, which is what the investigation part of this gig is all about." Financial relief always made me a bit more smug. And hungry. I took a cinnamon raisin bagel out of the bag and took a bite, and savored the sweet taste of success.

I finished my bagel and called the hospital to check up on Casey. The nurse at the desk who answered the phone made it sound like I was interrupting something important. I probably was, especially since it was the morning, and the hospital was probably short staffed, like every other hospital in western New York. She told me he was stable, and had a quiet night. Roughly translated from nurse-speak to English, no big changes one way or the other. Given the beating he took, I supposed that was good enough for now.

Sam usually brought in the newspaper in the mornings, so I grabbed it to check on the Dellaplante babies' funeral. According to the obituary notice, the funeral was to be at 11 o'clock at Our Lady of Perpetual Mercy. That was about an hour from now, which means I had a few hours before I could catch up with either Lawrence or Dellaplante. I have to admit I was torn between going to the funeral and all that would entail, and sneaking around to get at Lawrence. Remembering local tradition, I decided, after another bagel and more coffee, to call the Dellaplante Development yard I went to earlier.

"Good morning, Dellaplante Development!" chirped the perky voice on the other end of the line.

"Hey, yeah, good morning," I chimed in, smiling to sound a little happier than I was. "I was in there early this morning to see Mr. Lawrence, remember me?"

There was a strained silence on the other end of the line, as if the gears were turning before sudden revelation. "Oh yeah, hi! I remember you, are you still looking for Mikey? He's still not here, the funeral isn't 'til 11, and then there's the brunch after…"

"Oh yeah, that's right," I said. "About that. When I talked to Mike yesterday he told me I could meet him after the brunch, but I forgot where it was supposed to be. You know, I don't know what's happening to my memory these days."

"They say that happens as you get older," she giggled. "Oh, not that I think you're old or anything. You know, my dad started taking something that really helped him out. He's about your age and he

LAKE EFFECT

was forgetting everything all the time and my mom finally got so aggravated with him that she…"

"Anyway," I interrupted, completely derailing her train of thought, "did he mention where he was going after the funeral?"

"Oh yeah, I guess you would want to know that if you were gonna catch up with him."

"Exactly. Could you take a look for me and see if he wrote it down anywhere?"

"Oh sure, Mister, umm, you know I don't remember your name."

"Banks, Joe Banks. You can call me Joe if it makes it easier on you."

"Geez, I shoulda been able to remember that. Maybe I should get that memory stuff, too," she giggled again. "What was the name of it? Gildo, gecko, something…"

"Ginko biloba," I offered, not wanting her to hurt herself. "Were you able to find out where Mike was going after the funeral?"

"Oh yeah, just another second. Here it is! I guess everyone was meeting at Michael's in Hamburg. Isn't that funny! Meeting Mikey at Michael's!"

"Isn't it though," I went along. "This is great Miss, umm…"

"You can call me Cyndi, Joe, you know with the 'y' and the 'i' mixed up."

"I should have known," I said. "You have been a ton of help, Cyndi."

"No problem. I have to get back to work now, do you need anything else?"

"Nope, that should do it. I'll just plan on meeting Mike at Michael's." That sent her into another involuntary giggle.

"Okay then, nice talking to you, Joe. Ya know, you are a lot nicer than most of Mikey's friends that call here."

"I bet."

"Have a nice day, Joe."

"You too, Cyndi. Bye." I hung up, and reached into my desk for an aspirin.

Twelve

Thanks to my new friend Cyndi, I got to Michael's at about 12:30 in the afternoon. Michael's is a new banquet hall, owned by the same family that owns a very popular diner right next door. The place itself is well appointed, and elegantly, yet tastefully decorated. They seemed to do a especially good business, especially during peak prom and wedding season. Paula and I have been there a few times for weddings, christenings, and the like. There is a covered entrance, essential for the unpredictable western New York weather, and from my Jeep I could see the open, expansive foyer with its exceptionally large, exceedingly bright chandelier. There were several people milling around on the inside, dressed in dark colors. I could see Frank Dellaplante holding court, with his daughters by his side. He had his arm around Sharon, and appeared to be consoling her, her head buried in his right shoulder. Even from across a crowded foyer, she looked frail and worn by the whole ordeal.

I watched through a freezing drizzle as car after car pulled in, dropped off mourners and well-wishers, and proceeded to park out where the drivers could make a mad dash through the weather. I kept the engine running to keep the windshield warm enough to prevent ice from blocking my view. The parade slowed down a bit, when one of the cars took me by surprise. I watched as a familiar silver BMW pulled into parking lot. Kevin Garner took off like a stocky shot across the slick blacktop. He went over to Dellaplante immediately, shaking his hand, and then to Sharon, whom he gave a fatherly hug. This was getting interesting, so I decided to get out of the Jeep. I turned my collar up, ducked my head, and headed for the door.

Once inside, I turned the collar down on my pea coat, and handed it to the coat check girl. I was wearing a pair of black dress slacks and a black turtleneck, and was at least grateful my house was on the route to the banquet hall. I worked my way through the somber crowd towards Frank Dellaplante. Unfortunately, Maddy Dellaplante saw me first. She had looked sad, but seeing me changed all that.

"What the hell are you doing here?" she hissed angrily, straining to keep her composure. "Don't you think it's hard enough on Sharon without having some lowlife, parasitic asshole pushing his way into her privacy when she needs it the most?"

That hurt. I had never been called a parasite before. "Maddy, how good to see you again," I said, loudly enough for anyone close to hear. I watched her face blanch as I wrapped my arms around her and pulled her tightly to me. I whispered to her "Listen to me very carefully. I know you are trying to protect your sister, and so am I. I do not believe your sister was involved in this at all, and I want the guys who are. So get off my ass, and let me do my job and help your sister get her justice."

I let her go, and I could see the look of bewilderment on her face as I backed away. "If there is ever anything I can do, well, you know how to reach me," I said. She continued with her slack-jawed expression, and nodded slowly, perhaps understanding for the first time that I am not the bad guy she had hoped I would be. I guided her to one side and moved on towards her father.

As I moved towards Dellaplante, his eyes locked on mine. His stare was one of confusion and steely outrage. Once again I appeared to be unwelcome. I wasn't sure at all what it would take to make myself welcome, but I was getting used to it. As I came closer, his face darkened considerably. I smiled. "Frank," I said, "how are you holding up?"

"Mr. Banks, I am fine. May I ask what brings you here, today, now?" he asked through clenched teeth.

"Actually, Frank, I am here to make sure your daughter Sharon is okay, and then perhaps talk to someone who might not want her to be okay for very much longer."

"What are you talking about?" he demanded, taking me by the elbow to a more quiet section of the foyer. I went with him for a few steps, then stopped abruptly to catch him off guard. I spun quickly and stepped up to him.

"I told you when I took this case I would do what I felt I needed to do to find out what happened to your grandchildren. I found out

LAKE EFFECT

that your employee, Lawrence, was going to be here, and I needed to talk to him, the sooner the better. I am not here to upset anyone, and I will be out of here as soon as I possibly can be. Now you can either let me earn your money, or you can pay me for doing nothing. It's up to you. Frankly I'd rather be home drinking coffee and giving piggy back rides to a couple of adorable kids, but hey, that's just me."

He appeared to study my face to see if there was anything that would tell him I was insincere. There wasn't. Then, pulling in his teeth just a bit, he growled, "Do you know who Lawrence is? What he looks like?"

"Nope, but that's why I came to you first," I grinned. "By the way, Frank, do you know who the father is, and did he make it to the funeral?"

"Over there, by the banquet room doors, near Sharon. See the tall blonde guy, that's Lawrence. But please don't talk to him near her. She likes him, God only knows why, and I don't want her to know you're working for me. As for the father, well, Sharon was in her rebellious stage. I have my suspicions, but Sharon even went so far as to refuse to give a name for the birth certificate."

"Thanks," I said, and walked towards the banquet room. On my way, I found myself intercepted by Kevin Garner, whose beefy hand landed on my shoulder with a thud.

"Joe, what the hell are you doing here?" Kevin asked.

"My job, in spite of what a lot of people might think. I could ask you the same thing, Kev," I responded, turning slightly. I wanted to keep track of where Lawrence was.

"When the head of one of your larger corporate insurance accounts has a family tragedy, Kellerman believes the best thing to do is pretend like you care. Besides, I told you I was a friend of the family. So here I am, doing my job on behalf of Kellerman."

"No ass too big, no kiss too wet, huh?"

"Exactly. You got some big balls showing up here today, though. You had to come?" Kevin asked.

"Yeah, I think so. I have to talk to Michael Lawrence as soon as

79

possible, just so I can keep things moving. Here's as good a place as any, as far as I am concerned. I need to know what the deal is between he and Dellaplante," I explained.

"Good luck," Kevin said, "and please don't get into any trouble?"

"Naw, just a walk in the park," I said. I looked past him and towards the doorway where Lawrence stood with Sharon Dellaplante. They were still talking, him smiling at her as she looked down at the floor. Her shoulders were rounded, hunched with her arms folded across her stomach. As they talked, he would occasionally lift her chin, gently, as if to get her to look at him instead of her shoes. She would, but only for the briefest of moments. Then she would look down again, apparently defeated by her own grief. And from where I was standing, Lawrence looked to me like he was trying to console her. For the first time even I began to feel like I was in the wrong place at the wrong time.

I waited, hiding in the crowd of family and friends, until he finally moved away from Sharon. She didn't need to know I was there, and I needed to get to Lawrence. He proceeded to the men's room, and I slipped through the assembly and followed him in a minute or two later. He was washing his hands when I entered the room, and decided not to waste time or words.

"Michael Lawrence?" I asked. He stood a few inches taller than me, and maybe a few pounds heavier because of it. There was no sign of paunch on the boy, and his build was more athletic than truly muscular. Frankly, a specimen of genetics gone horribly right.

"Yes, I'm Mike Lawrence. Do I know you?" he asked. He looked at me curiously, like a fighter or a wrestler studying an opponent. He was wary without knowing why, yet.

"Mr. Lawrence, my name is Banks," I said, handing him my business card. "I have been hired to look into the murder of Sharon Dellaplante's children."

"Aren't the police doing that already?" asked Lawrence, reading the card. "Who would waste the money and hire a private eye to do the work the cops are doing already? No offense meant."

"None taken," I replied. "And unfortunately, I can't exactly

LAKE EFFECT

answer that. I was wondering, since this isn't the time or the place obviously, if I could meet with you later to talk, find out what I can."

"Sure, I guess. Why don't you call my secretary Cyndi at..."

I held my hand up. "No offense to you, but I've already met Cyndi. If you don't mind, I'd rather talk directly with you to set this up. I'm sure she's good at what she does, whatever that may be. But this is very important, and I don't trust her to get the message straight."

Lawrence chuckled. "I know, but she's loyal to a fault. When do you want to meet and where?"

We agreed to meet late that afternoon at a coffee and doughnut shop in West Seneca. We also agreed not to say anything to Sharon, so we would not upset her further. Satisfied that I got what I came for, I went for my coat. On my way to the coat check room, Frank Dellaplante approached me at a trot. "Did you find him, did you scare him off, threaten him to leave my daughter alone?" he asked, huffing.

"Oh yeah, left him a quaking mass in the rest room, Frank," I said. "I will talk him into submission later, maybe use a rubber hose to beat a contrite confession from him, and send you the video of the whole process for your library later." I don't know what it is about that guy, but he always brings out the sarcasm in me. Which always seemed to bring out the very best in him, too.

"Don't forget who's paying you, you smug son of a bitch," he said, his face reddening with anger. "I want him to pay for what he's done to my little girl, and to my grandkids!"

"I was wondering Frank, have you actually ever seen them together? I mean watched them, noticed how they behave? It might surprise you."

"I don't have to watch a cobra to know how deadly it is, Banks. He is using her, manipulating her to get to me, to bring me down. I know it. I need you to prove it, but if that is too much for you, just say so. I know others who would be happy to do the work you can't."

I sighed. "Frank, you hired me to do a job. I do it my way, the best way I know how. When you are ready to take advice on how to

81

shortcut building codes from me, I will be happy to learn all of your vast knowledge of investigation, okay?" That managed to raise a few eyebrows in those close enough to eavesdrop, and from the looks of the vein pulsing in his forehead, it managed to raise his blood pressure a few dozen points. My work then was complete. I turned my back on the fuming Dellaplante, got my coat from the coat check girl, and tipped her well. After all, I was having a really good day.

Thirteen

I arrived at Tim Horton's at 4:45 in the afternoon, and it was already dark. For my part, I liked to arrive early when possible. It gives me the opportunity to observe whomever it is I'm meeting, to see what they do when they walk into an uncertain situation. Sometimes that's a good thing to know, so I try to find out when I can. About 10 minutes later Michael Lawrence came through the door, dressed in his black suit, black overcoat, looking like everyone's All American in mourning. I stood up so he could see me. He nodded, and came to the table. I put out my hand, and he shook it firmly.

"I'm glad you could make it," I said. "We have to talk, and I need some answers."

"Mr. Banks, I think I should let you know that you aren't the only one looking for answers," he replied, sitting. "I have done a little homework since we met this afternoon. I know, for instance that you are working for Kellerman Insurance on behalf of your old friend Kevin Garner. I know that you have spoken to almost every member of the Dellaplante family with the exception of Frank's wife."

"Congratulations, you have done some homework. I'm impressed," I said.

"I also know your reputation, that when you were a cop you never knew to leave well enough alone, and that almost got you killed. And you never let anyone or anything keep you from finding out the truth. That makes you either committed or a hard-ass."

"You can make the call on your own" I replied.

"And I know that you are giving old man Dellaplante apoplexy because he can't buy you off or threaten you," he said.

"I'm also loyal, thrifty and trustworthy. I still have a problem with obedient, but I'm working on it."

That brought a laugh, and we both relaxed a little. "So now that we understand a little bit about each other," I said, taking a sip of coffee, "do you mind if I ask you a few questions?"

"I suppose so. I want the same thing you want, to find out what happened to my, those two kids," he said, catching himself.

"Come again?"

"I said I want to find out who killed those kids…"

"No, you said my, my two kids." He squirmed a little, and looked everywhere but at me, like a little boy who got caught with his hand in the cookie jar. I kept my gaze on him, and he finally smiled at me.

"Okay, my kids okay. Sharon and I are more than just friends, as you have probably guessed," he said awkwardly. "Her old man freaked when she got pregnant with David when we were dating, so he forbid her from ever seeing me again. That worked for a little while, while I was in college, but when I came back to town, we got back together. One thing led to another and along came our beautiful Sarah." His voice began to crack, and his eyes misted and filled. He sniffed hard to regain his composure. "Sharon never told her father I was the father of the babies, so he naturally assumed she didn't know. I can only imagine what he thought of her then. In his mind, that made getting pregnant her way of rebelling against him for trying to get rid of me. The asshole has the most wonderful woman for a daughter, and like everything else in his life he takes her for granted, like that's the way it's supposed to be."

Lawrence was starting to get loud, and emotional, and that made me a bit nervous, so I put my hand on his forearm to calm him. He realized what he was doing, and brought himself under control. "So what happened the night of the carjacking, Michael," I asked him quietly.

He took a deep breath and started. "Sharon took the kids to do a little Christmas shopping. Last minute stuff, you know, stocking stuffers, and things like that. I had been working a lot of hours for Dellaplante, and saved enough money to make for a very special Christmas for the kids and Sharon. All the big presents were bought, but at the last minute, Sharon told me she had a few things to pick up, and wanted to get out with the kids. I was at the trailer, so I gave the kids a kiss, told them I loved them, and did the same to Sharon, and told her I was going to go home to prep for a zoning meeting the next day."

"Anyway I was home, about 11 o'clock I guess, when I got a

LAKE EFFECT

phone call from Sharon. She was at the Cheektowaga Police station, screaming they took the kids, and stole her van, and could I come get her. I did, and she told me some black guys jumped her from behind as she was getting in the driver's side. The cops questioned her, but it was dark, and she said the guys had ski masks on so she didn't get a real good look at them. Since then we have been devastated, and I'll admit even the old man was crushed. He still went storming around the office, but tended to run out of steam faster. I tried to pretend it was business as usual, and offered to help Dellaplante and his family anyway I could. Some of the office staff thought I was kissing up, but it was my way to try and stay close to Sharon if she needed me."

"So what happened when they found the van?" I asked.

"I was with Sharon when they found the van, and she just broke down completely. Lost it, you know, was inconsolable. I held it together as best I could, for her sake, but it was like somebody ripped out my heart and stepped on it until it quit beating. We called her sister Maddy, and she came over and started helping with the funeral arrangements. We tried to reach her father, but he was nowhere to be found for the next day or so. We finally did reach him, and told him what happened. He wanted to know if anyone was caught, and after we told him no, he asked how Sharon was. Once again, an afterthought."

"Not a lot of love lost between you and Dellaplante," I observed.

"None. Maybe we got along okay at first, but now, we tolerate each other, at best. At worst, well...," he trailed off, shrugging.

"We've been sitting here talking, in a coffee shop, and we have no coffee in front of us," I said, breaking the tension a bit. "I'm gonna get a cup, want some?"

"Yeah, sure, black please."

I walked up to the counter and placed my order. As the counter girl went to get the coffee, I turned back towards the table and watched Lawrence. His upright posture gave way to a flat slouch, with his chin buried in his chest. I suspected he was the father of the two kids, but I also suspected him to be a cocky, absentee type who didn't

85

give a damn, especially after what Sharon said about him when we met. I assumed it was an act. It was almost heartbreaking to watch a guy who said he loved his babies as much as their mother grieve so secretly. I paid for the coffee, and carried them back to the table. I put one cup in front of Lawrence and he stared at it for a moment lost in thought. I pulled my chair out and sat across from him and watched as he took a long slow turn at his coffee. I took a sip of mine, and sighed audibly.

Finally, I said, "At least the insurance money will help Sharon out of that trailer park she's living in."

"What money?" he said, not looking up. "Neither Sharon nor I could afford insurance on ourselves, much less the kids. Besides, who ever expects babies to die?"

"Nobody, I guess," I replied, warily.

"What made you say that Mr. Banks. I mean, about the insurance?"

"C'mon, Mike. You're a smart guy, and at the very least inquisitive. You want me to believe you know nothing about the insurance policy on David and Sarah? You'll have to do a little better than that," I said, hoping to draw him out.

He looked at me warily. I could tell he was being cautious about his next response. He looked down, took a sip of coffee, and then fixed his gaze on me. "I hope you don't think I'm trying to be evasive. I do know what you're talking about, but I'm not sure about you, and you're not sure about me yet. I have never lost anything being careful."

"Careful is good, but let's not waste a lot of each other's time," I replied. "Someone killed your son and your daughter, and for a lot of reasons I am committed to find out who, and why, and I have no desire to screw around about it. You are either going to help me, or you're going to get in my way. If you decide not to help me, and get in the way, I will make sure you are never going to be eligible for father of the year. Now are we going to talk, or what?" Lawrence's face darkened, as if I had touched a raw nerve, and ripped it out.

It took him a moment to regain his composure. I was waiting for

LAKE EFFECT

the normal color to return to his face when he said weakly, "I knew about the policy, but I never thought he would, I mean what kind of human would kill for money?"

"What are you talking about, Mike?" I asked. "Who's 'he'?"

"Old man Dellaplante. He bought the insurance policies on the kids. I had been auditing the company's expenses, and found out Dellaplante Development was paying for the policies, and one on Sharon, too. Did you know she is covered for a half a million?"

I nodded in silence. I was content to let him think I knew more than I did. He took another sip and said, "The company was losing money, a lot of it, and we were busier than ever. I mean, we had projects going on all over the place, and more and more of them were not even bid jobs. People were coming to us to do their renovations, or their new builds, or whatever. But still, every time I looked we were losing money on every project. So as I was digging into why, checking out all the places we were having cost over runs, I came across this entry in the general ledger as an additional payment to Kellerman Insurance. You have a friend that works for them, don't you?" he asked rhetorically.

Once again I nodded. "Yes, I do," I replied flatly. I was trying to remain inscrutable. No reason, just practice.

He shifted nervously, as his attempt to surprise me with his own investigation failed. "Yeah, well, anyway," he began again, "I saw the entry and at first I thought it was just another property casualty payment, or Worker's Compensation premium payment. But it was out of the usual sequence so I checked into it further. It was to pay for one year's premium on a life insurance policy on Sharon, and one on David and Sarah as well. I thought it was a gift of some sort, though I don't know too many people that look at a life insurance policy as the perfect gift."

I smiled, and said, "The rich are different."

"I have started to figure that out."

"What else did you find, Mike?"

"I thought we were just talking about the life insurance."

"We were. Now we're not. What else did you find?"

He swallowed hard. "What makes you think I found anything else?"

"Michael, really, what makes you think that you could keep anything from me? I thought we'd gotten past all the silly games of 'I've Got A Secret'." I was bluffing, but I needed to know everything, and he was holding out on me.

He shook his head. "I don't want to wind up half dead in Mercy Hospital like that beach rat did," he said, fear starting to fill his eyes. That surprised me, but I tried not to let him know.

"Of course you don't, but who's to say that won't happen anyway just from our having this little heart to heart. Talk to me, tell me something I can use to help nail the people who killed David and Sarah."

He stared steadily into his coffee cup while he spoke. "I started looking over the past few years, back to 1997, when we first started losing money on jobs. I looked at labor costs, materials, bonds, anything I could think of. Finally, I reviewed the miscellaneous items in the budget, and found that a significant amount of money was being sent to NPA Productions on Grand Cayman Island, a gambling web site. You know the kind of place, online casino gaming, sports betting, anything else you want to bet on, they'll cover it. I looked deeper and found that he built some of the money into the travel and entertainment line on the bids. Dellaplante Development was missing bids because the travel and entertainment budgets were too high. After a few dozen lost bid reviews, and even more over-budget projects, I found they all had varying amounts going to NPA Productions."

"Did you bring it to Dellaplante's attention?"

"I did. He blew it off, didn't even acknowledge there was a problem."

"Interesting."

Lawrence looked at me like I was crazy for a second, but then continued. It almost seemed like he needed to tell someone this, needed to let someone else in on the secret. I couldn't tell if he was trying to protect himself by sharing the story, or trying to hurt his

LAKE EFFECT

employer. "Anyway, he said that we had plenty of work coming in so we shouldn't have any problems covering the losses from the 'less profitable projects'. It was almost as if he considered his gambling debts a cost of doing business," Lawrence said.

"I started making copies of the documents that I found, making sure that if anything happened I would have a way to cover myself. I didn't want to catch any heat for this guy, not if I could avoid it."

I leaned back in my chair, crossed my arms and said, "You know, your actions could be interpreted differently, don't you?"

"What do you mean? All I am trying to do here is help you out and cover my own ass," he said excitedly.

"From the outside, you could be trying to put together the goods on your boss, maybe take him down a little. You know, blackmail him to keep you quiet about his business practices. Wouldn't be the first time in history a disgruntled employee tried to get over on his boss," I explained quietly.

"Is that what you are accusing me of?" he asked, his neck straining as his face began to turn red.

"No," I said, "I'm not accusing you of anything. In fact, all I was doing is telling how things can look differently than they really are. Unless I can prove otherwise, I have to believe you're telling me the truth."

Suddenly, Lawrence stared right past me, his pupils dilating, all the color running from his face. What was once a face of rage became suddenly a face of shock and fear. I spun around in my chair looking towards the full pane window that looked out at the parking lot and saw someone spin away from the glass and take off at a dead run towards an old Ford 150 pickup truck. All I could make out was a royal blue baseball cap, a black Buffalo Sabres jacket, and a pair of blue jeans. I never saw his face, but Lawrence did. I turned back to him, and said, "Who was that, Mike?"

"Nobody," he said curtly, looking at his watch. "Look, I have to go. If you need to talk to me again, well, you're the detective, you can find me." If that was an attempt at humor, he really should stick to his day job.

RONALD W. ADAMS

"Right. By the way, you're not afraid of 'Nobody', are you?" I asked after him. He had his overcoat on and was well on his way to the door, but that caught his attention. He said nothing, but shot me the look. Good comeback.

Fourteen

It was about 6:30 pm by the time I got home. Supper was a warm plate in the oven, and I ate quickly as Kyle and Amanda colored pictures with Paula in the family room. I took the plate to the sink, rinsed it off, and joined the rest of the art class. Paula was great with art, and even dabbled in painting classes in oils, pastels and acrylics before we got the kids. She has a fantastic sense of color, proportion, and fun, whereas all my pictures never made it past the level of fifth grade, back of the school book scribbling. Kyle wanted nothing to do with any of the other colors except for blue, which suited Amanda just fine. That just meant more crayons for her.

"Catch the bad guys yet?" Paula asked playfully.

"Still trying to figure out who the bad guys are," I replied, trying to draw a circle in blue crayon for Kyle.

"Sounds like a productive day." My wife has a gift for sarcasm.

"Uh-huh, just another day in paradise. I did manage to get some answers, though, and discovered I was one of the least welcome guests at the funeral of the Dellaplante children."

"How did that go?" Paula asked, looking up from her Crayola still life, handing the yellow crayon to Amanda. We walked in to the kitchen adjacent to the family room, so we could talk and keep an eye on the kids at the same time.

"Uncomfortable, and intrusive, especially on my part. But I think I really made an impression on Maddy Dellaplante, and managed to surprise Frank. And I got to meet and talk with Michael Lawrence."

"Who?"

"Lawrence works for Dellaplante. Turns out he is the dead kids' father, and that he has some dirt on Frank and Dellaplante Development. We were having this really nice conversation, baring our souls like two guys in a coffee shop do, you know. Then somebody spooked him, really bad. I never got a good look at him, and I wasn't able to go after him, but it shut Lawrence up completely. It was weird."

"What do you mean?" Paula asked nervously. She always had a

look of concern when she heard me talk about some of the less comfortable parts of the job. She told me once not knowing was worse, because her imagination was generally worse than any reality I faced.

"It was as if somebody wanted him to know they were watching him, and they could get to him if they wanted to. And he apparently got the message."

Paula looked down. "And if they know how to get to him, and they know who you are, will they know how to get to you, too?" she asked in hushed tones.

The answer was probably yes. "I don't know, hon," I told her, hoping to give her some kind of comfort.

"Should I call my cousin, Carrie? I could take the kids and stay with her for a few days if we have to," she said.

"That's a little premature I think," I told her, still wanting to make her feel like she was safe in her own home.

"Really?"

"Yeah, I think so. It's probably nothing for us to worry about. If they wanted to send me a message, it would have been a lot more direct." I hugged her and kissed her forehead.

Amanda came in to the kitchen with her yellow crayon, and tugged at Paula's pant leg. "Mamma, you have to draw with me, please?"

We smiled at each other, and Paula took Amanda by the hand and went back to the family room. I stood in the doorway, soaking in the domestic tranquility of it all. The nasty business of the Dellaplante family faded a little watching Paula, with little Kyle on her lap, and Amanda diligently working on her latest refrigerator masterpiece. Times like these disappear too quickly, and come too far between.

Bedtime for the munchkins came at 8:30 pm, and Paula and I were left to clean up the aftermath of a hard day at play. Once the toys were put in their respective toy boxes, we stalled out beside each other on the couch, hands held tightly. We flipped through the channels on the television, and discovered absolutely nothing. We turned to each other, smiled, and turned off the TV. Paula kissed my ear playfully, and whispered, "Good idea." We managed to exchange

LAKE EFFECT

a lot of good ideas on the couch. There was a deep comfort in knowing that, even fifteen years later, we could still make love like when we met, and we didn't have to make love to prove how we felt about each other.

About 11:30 pm, Paula decided to turn in for the night. I felt too wired, and probably would have just laid there tossing and turning, so I decided to catch the late news, and go over my notes on the Dellaplante case. I turned off the outside lights on the garage and the front porch, and had turned out the lights in family room. Our house was deceptive, because with the family room lights out, and the nightlight we kept on in the kitchen, it was hard to tell from the outside if anyone was awake or not inside. We used to have an alarm system, and, while we live in a quiet subdivision, it did give us some minor peace of mind. But after a while, feeling safe and secure, we stopped using it. It became just an unnecessary expense, and we really didn't need any extra frills in our already tight budget. So when I heard the first thud coming from the back of the garage, I started wishing that we kept the alarm connected.

On the side of the garage near the back, Paula and I had the builder install a door so that we could have a second entrance from the back yard, behind the stockade fence. At the first noise, I got up, and moved to the pantry in the kitchen. We keep a full size MagLite there in case of blackouts. It is long and black and hefty in your hand, a heavy-duty light for heavy-duty work. I pulled it out and moved out of the kitchen and into the front hallway as the back door between the mudroom and the garage opened with a metallic pop. My pulse raced as I heard the first footsteps from the mudroom and into the kitchen. I waited with the flashlight down at my side in my right hand, back against the hall wall, barely breathing.

I watched, eyes adjusted to the dark, and listened as the footsteps approached closer and closer. The intruder wore soft-soled shoes that were wet, and squeaked slightly on the linoleum. I saw the barrel of a pistol come into view, followed by a gloved hand, and a pair of black jacketed forearms as the prowler continued to move forward. As soon as I saw his elbows, I brought the flashlight up

RONALD W. ADAMS

hard and fast around the corner, and felt the steel hit something hard that gave way under the force of the blow. I came around the corner as fast as the flashlight did and grabbed the hand holding the gun, twisting it down and away. The hand hit the island counter, and the gun skidded across the floor towards the sink. I continued forward and wound up straddling the intruder, sitting on his chest as his free hand covered his face, blood oozing from between the fingers. I looked down and saw the red and silver Buffalo Sabres logo on the left side of the chest. Looking at me was the man whom I had seen at the Tim Horton's with Lawrence. Behind me the kitchen light came on, and I could hear Paula say, "Oh my God, Joe..."

"Honey, go back up to our room and call the cops, and an ambulance," I said as calmly as I could. I noticed the left sleeve of his black jacket was ripped at the shoulder seam.

"An ambulance? Are you hurt?" she asked nervously.

"It's not for me," I said, grabbing the stranger's already bleeding nose and twisting it to the sound of a grown man's screams. As he howled and reached again for his nose, I drove my fist hard into his hands. His eyes rolled back into his head as he lost consciousness.

"Quiet," I said, "you'll wake the kids."

Fifteen

The police gave me the option to go to the station that night or to swear out a complaint in the morning, and I decided to wait until then. The rest of the night was spent holding my sobbing wife, convincing her I was all right, and having her hate my job all over again. The kids slept right through the excitement, thankfully. We talked for a while as neither one of us was able to sleep very well. It was decided, for her safety and for the kids, maybe home wasn't the place to be. At first we thought they would be able to stay with her cousins Mark and Deanna at their farm out in Fredonia. It was quiet and definitely out of the way. However, we thought the better of it since they had just returned from China a few days earlier with their new daughter. Having 'been there-done that' ourselves with Kyle and Amanda, we understood how the first few days are, and they needed a little adjustment time. Paula then called her cousin Carrie, who also lived off the beaten path in the town of Orchard Park. After explaining things to her, Carrie said she would be happy to take in the crew for a few days.

In the morning, I helped Paula pack a few things for her stay with Carrie, and got the kids ready for the 'big sleepover party at Aunt Carrie's house'.

"Finish this thing, Joe. I want my home back," Paula said, folding some clothes for the kids. She zipped up the duffel bag she was packing and handed it to me.

"Tell Carrie I said thank you for taking care of you and the kids," I told her, and gave her a kiss. Kyle and Amanda came running over and each grabbed a leg and held on tightly.

"We goin' Aunt Carrie house, Dad. You go, too?" Kyle asked, with his bright smile and shining blue eyes. "You go, too?"

"Pleathe," Amanda pleaded with her almost irresistible lisp, hoping we could all go and have fun at Aunt Carrie's. They were a two-child conspiracy to break me down. I knelt down and hugged them both tightly, eyes closed. Kyle squeezed me around the neck, and Amanda patted my shoulder as she hugged me back.

"Daddy has to work, guys. But you are gonna have big fun with Mommy and Aunt Carrie for the next day or so," I told them, then kissed their foreheads.

Amanda smiled and chimed in, "And buttafly kisses too, Dadda." We rubbed noses back and forth, and she giggled.

"Dadda go work now, catch bad guys," Kyle stated, very matter of factly. I wished I shared an ounce of his conviction and confidence.

"Yup," I said.

"Like Batman," he said, beaming proudly.

"Yeah, just like Batman."

And with that the two of them ran over to Paula, who scooped them up and took them to her van. We loaded them into the car seats, and gave them each a toy to play with. Sliding the doors shut, we met at the driver's side door, kissed and held each other for a minute. There wasn't much that needed to be said that we didn't already know.

"I love you, and I'll be careful," I said.

"I know, and me too," she said, tears beginning to well in her beautiful brown eyes.

She backed the van out of the driveway, and left to Carrie's house. I shut the garage door, and went into the basement to the fireproof safe we keep in the back corner of the farthest wall from the stairs. We bought the safe originally for important documents – life insurance, adoption documents, birth certificates and the like. They were housed in another safe now in the attic. This safe in the basement held something else. Opening it, I removed a shoulder holster, still a light tan and a little stiff from the amount of use it didn't get. Reaching in again I removed a Colt .45 caliber semi-automatic pistol, and 4 loaded clips of ammunition. I carefully inspected the gun, inserted a clip, and chambered the first round. I set the safety, and put it in the holster, strapping it down. I carried the other clips with me upstairs, and put them in the pocket of my coat. I hated to carry the gun because it was a heavy reminder of the type of work I do, and the type of people I really have to deal with, but I promised to be careful and I had every intention of keeping that promise.

LAKE EFFECT

I drove to the Hamburg Police station about 9:30, and saw the desk sergeant who guided me fortunately to the desk of Detective Jimmy Ramone. Jimmy was a townie, born and raised and lived all of his 35 years in Hamburg. He was a skinny guy, but wiry and quick. He had his dark hair in a crew cut, and was just starting to show gray at the top. His eyes were dark brown, almost black, and intensely curious. Ramone knew me from other jobs I had done, and, unlike some cops, knew he didn't have all the answers when it came to private guys like me. He was a straight shooter, with an attitude that said to everyone he was his own man. I respected him, and the respect was mutual. We shook hands as I sat down in front of his desk.

"Hey Joe, I thought you never brought work home with you," he said laughing.

"I just love my job so much Jimmy," I joked back. My coat opened slightly as I sat, and he spotted the gun in the holster.

"If I remember correctly, that's not your style," he commented, pointing.

"It isn't, but I promised Paula I would be more careful," I told him. "Truth be told I haven't even broken in the holster in two years."

"So what happened? Beside the obvious, I mean."

I told him a little about the case, hoping maybe he could help. Then I told him about seeing the guy outside Tim Horton's while interviewing Michael Lawrence. "Then the sonovabitch shows up in my house. I don't know how he looks today, but I have a feeling he's sorry he took that little job," I said.

Ramone looked up from his notes at me, smiling. "What did you hit him with?" he asked, snickering.

"MagLite," I said, raising one eyebrow.

Ramone grinned and nodded. "Go on."

"That's it. He passed out, and was out like a light, no pun intended, when the cops got there."

"Joe, the guy had a friggin' concussion when we locked him up."

"Well I have been lifting two year olds a lot lately, you know, working out."

"We have to talk to him yet, especially in light of everything you told me. You think somebody paid him to scare you?"

"Absolutely."

"Any idea who?"

"I figure somebody who doesn't want the Dellaplante case solved, but nobody I can point a finger to yet."

"You mean you haven't solved it yet. Geez, you must really suck at this. That Spenser guy in Boston used to solve all his mysteries in an hour on TV," Ramone said sarcastically.

"That's because I don't work with a big, bald, black guy. And I don't look anything like Robert Urich."

"You have a point. You want to watch how real policemen do their job?"

"Why? Is *Dragnet* on?" I shot back.

We walked down the stairs to the lower floor of the building, and into the holding area. A uniformed officer, who looked like he'd almost rather be out on traffic duty than watching a holding tank, met us. He opened the door to the cell, and Ramone led the way in. I stood in the background. My midnight visitor was sitting on a bench, head hanging down. The guy was smaller, thinner than I recall him being from last night, but it was dark. He was still wearing the Sabres jacket, but with what I would assume was a brand new blood stain on the collar and chest of it. He was also accessorized with a bandage that took up the majority of the middle of his face. It was stained a dark red from the draining and dried blood from his nose. He looked up, his brown hair short but greasy, like he hadn't showered after a lot of sweat. His eyes were half shut, black and blue and swollen. He looked at both of us, then looked twice at me, and hung his head back down. The uniformed officer brought us a pair of folding chairs, and we unfolded them and set them on the concrete floor with a clank. Ramone turned his chair backwards and sat on it facing the sad-faced kid. I was more traditional, and sat back with my arms folded.

"Mr. Banks, meet Victor Maloney. Oh, wait, that's right, you

LAKE EFFECT

two have met before," he chimed sarcastically.

"I don't believe we have ever been formally introduced," I said, keeping up the act. I smiled at him, and he grunted something incoherently.

"Mr. Banks, I do believe Mr. Maloney said it is a pleasure to make your acquaintance, though I am sure he wishes it were not under such unpleasant circumstances. Isn't that right, Victor?" he said, not so much as a question but as a statement of fact.

"I wanna talk to my lawyer," he blurted out in a very nasal intonation.

"What?" Ramone asked. "Is that one of those goofy Boston accents? Mr. Banks, you're from that area of the country, do you know what Mr. Maloney here is trying to say?"

The kid looked at me, and I shot him a smile back. "I could be wrong, but I believe he has asked to see his attorney, Detective Ramone."

"Oh yes, he does have that right, of course. Does that mean you want us to call him for you, or do you want to talk to him yourself?"

"I'll call him, you bring me the phone," he responded.

"But that means I have to leave Mr. Banks alone in a semi-dark room with you, Victor. You wouldn't try to hurt him again, would you, Victor?" Ramone was getting up from the chair, when Maloney stood up first.

"You can't, I mean, he's not a cop, he's just a P.I. for chrissake. You can't leave him alone in a cell with me."

"Victor, I am surprised!," Ramone exclaimed, his hands shooting to his cheeks for mock emphasis. "You must be one of those jailhouse lawyers I've heard so much about. And so well informed regarding the rights and responsibilities of the citizens of Hamburg." His face suddenly became very serious. "How do you know what Mr. Banks does for a living, Victor?"

"From you, you must have said something when you first got here," Victor stammered.

"Guess again, Vic," I said, still smiling like the Cheshire cat. He was starting to get nervous, and I was truly starting to enjoy it.

99

"You can't leave him here with me," Victor whined. I hate whining.

"Victor, I'm sure you and Mr. Banks have lots to discuss," Ramone said, opening the cell door. "I'll be right back with your phone."

Victor shot a pleading look at the cell door, and then back at me. I smiled and stood up. I moved my chair across the room, closer to Victor. I sat back down, leaning forward with my elbows on my knees. "Hi Vic. Remember me?"

"I don't have to say anything until my lawyer gets here," Victor mumbled.

"Nope you don't have to say anything to the cops until your lawyer gets here. Funny thing about that, though. I'm not a cop. I'm the guy whose house you broke into last night, who lost a night's sleep talking to the cops and scrubbing your blood off my kitchen floor. So I'm tired, I'm grumpy, and I'm in no mood to dick around with a loser like you. So talk to me. Now!"

"Bite me, Banks. You don't scare me with your act," Maloney replied, the tough guy act severely impaired by his newly nasal voice. It reminded me of Henry Aldrich of the old time radio programs. My right hand shot out and grabbed his nose through the bandage and squeezed hard. I could feel the bandage becoming wet and warm under my fingers. His pupils dilated and his face blanched, and his mouth opened in a silent scream.

"That was not very nice. Let me put it to you this way. I'm a very reasonable person, with very reasonable expectations from other people. Therefore, I reasonably expect us to be alone in this room for a little while. Let's try to make the best of a really bad situation. Shall we?"

He nodded in silent agreement. I continued, "I know your face hurts, and your nose is broken, and it is probably very difficult to talk in more than one word sentences, so we will keep this very simple and straightforward. Did someone pay you to keep an eye on Michael Lawrence?"

His hands covered his face, but he managed to nod yes. "Did that same someone pay you to break into my house?"

LAKE EFFECT

He hesitated, then shook his head, his eyes opening as wide as they could.

"Victor, we were doing so well. Did the same person pay you to break into my house?" I asked insistently, leaning closer to his already very sensitive face. This time he nodded in the affirmative.

"Were you there to hurt me, or my family?"

He pointed at me.

"Who is it, Victor?"

He shook his head.

"Don't know or won't say?"

"Don't know," he grunted. "Guy calls, gives me the job, cash goes into the bank direct."

Neat and clean, I thought to myself. "Who set you up with the phone calls?"

"This guy I met at some hole in the wall bar in the University District, near campus. We got talking, he asked me about money for school..."

"Money for school?"

"Yeah, I'm in my third year pre-law at U.B. Funny, huh?" he said, pulling his hands away from his face.

"Ironic, if nothing else. You know me, you know what I do, and you know who I do it for?"

"The way I heard it you're the private eye working on the Dellaplante babies case."

"That's right. You got anything to add to that?" I asked him.

"Just what I read in the papers, I guess. Dead babies, grieving parents, all very sad." Spoken like a smarmy lawyer already.

"So what were you doing in my house you smart-assed son of a bitch? Were you trying to hurt me, scare me, or kill me?" I slid the chair forward and pinned his knees between the chair and the cot. He grunted slightly.

"The guy who called, he said you have a rep for being hard headed, but if I could get to your wife or kids, you'd cave and give it up." He looked passed me nervously towards the door. "Hey, where's that cop friend of yours with that phone? I shouldn't be talking to you at

101

all, but you aren't a cop, so I can say whatever and it don't matter.
You can't do shit about it, Banks." He chuckled nervously. "My
attorney will have me outta here in time for classes."

"You know what, you're probably right. And of course, you'll be
free on bail pending trial, and there's not much I can do about it.
That is, if I was a cop. But as you were so quick to point out, I'm not
a cop, am I?" His facial expression changed from confidence to
concern. "And now that we know each other, you shouldn't be all
that hard to find, if we need to talk again that is."

"What do you mean if we need to talk?"

"You know, if anything comes up I need to know about, anything
I don't understand, anything doesn't make sense, things like that.
It's not often I can take advantage of the insight of a third year pre-
law student from U.B." He stared at me for a moment, as if I was
slightly out of my mind. "Unless of course there's some reason you
wouldn't want to be seen with me. It wouldn't hurt your social
standing, would it? You, a third year law student and wanna-be bad
guy, and me a nasty old private eye, do you think your friends might
see us and get the wrong idea?"

"N-n-no, I guess not," he stammered nervously.

"Unless, maybe…no, probably not, but you never know."

"Know what?" he pleaded.

"Maybe, the guy who paid you to watch me, and Michael
Lawrence, paid someone else to watch you. Do you think he would?"
I asked him innocently. I do innocent well, if I do say so myself.

"Wh-why would he do that?" he asked innocently, but not as
innocently as me.

"Well, real bad guys, not guys like you but the real kind, will
keep an eye on a weak link if they think he may break. Especially if
the wanna-be bad guy spent the night in jail, and had been visited by
the guy he was told to threaten. Who knows what could happen?"

Just then Jimmy Ramone came to the cell, dragging a phone to
the door. Saved by Ma Bell. The guard opened the door and the
phone was handed to Victor, who requested a little privacy to call
his lawyer. Jimmy and I walked back to his office, where I took a

LAKE EFFECT

small micro-cassette recorder out of the inside pocket of my jacket. After checking the sound on the tape, I rewound it, popped it out of the machine, and handed it to him.

"Hope this helps. Now I have a couple of favors to ask you," I said, sitting in front of his desk.

"As long as they're reasonable," Ramone said, "go ahead."

"First, I want a copy of Victor's mug shot to flash by a couple of guys from the boat launch. They came in and some of your men gave them a bad time," I told him. "Be easier if I took it to them."

"Done. And?" he asked.

"We share information, okay? I find out something, I come to you. And if you find something, you let me know. Deal?"

"That's fair. You know that with no priors and a well to do family, Victor's gonna make bail," Ramone pointed out.

"I'd be surprised if he didn't. But with any luck at all, maybe that can work to our advantage," I said with a smile.

Sixteen

It was starting to snow big puffy flakes, enough to cover the dingy, black tinged snow piles but not enough to make driving a nuisance. No matter how much winter we seem to get around here, people still refer to this kind of snowfall as pretty. I left the Hamburg Police station and was on my way to Mercy Hospital, armed with a picture of my new best friend Victor Maloney. I had assumed the Bowery Boys, also known as Herbie and Mickey, would be there to visit Casey, and would be able to take a look at the picture. My keen sense of detecting was telling me that this Victor fellow knew significantly more than he was letting on.

I pulled into the visitor's parking lot at Mercy Hospital just before visiting hours began. As I suspected, I spotted Herbie and Mickey furiously inhaling on the last of their cigarettes before going up to visit their friend Casey. I parked the Jeep, locked it, and jogged a little to catch up with them. They grunted and nodded their greetings in unison. I had to suppress a chuckle at the way great minds worked alike. I reached into my upper coat pocket and pulled out the mug shot of my wanna-be burglar Victor. "Does this guy look familiar to either of you," I asked, showing them the photo.

"Sort of," said Mickey, holding the picture between his nicotine stained fingers. "But it looks like someone took a ball bat to his face, man."

Herbie took it next. "Jesus," he exclaimed, "who messed up this poor bastard?"

"Guilty," I said. "I need you guys to take a good look at him. Was he one of the guys you saw at the landing the night they dumped the van in the lake?"

They continued to peer at the picture, straining their memories to see if they had seen him before. They were right about one thing. The damage done by the flashlight was not going to make it easy to identify him. Herbie looked up from the picture, and asked me, "What the hell happened to this guy's face, man? What did you do him like that for?"

"For breaking into my house," I said coldly. "For breaking in and threatening my family. How's Casey doing? Is he still in ICU?"

Mickey coughed a deep phlegmy cough and spit some brown mucous on the ground to the side of him. "Yeah," he barked, "they say he ain't doin' too good. You think the punk in the picture is involved at all with them kids or with Casey?"

"I'm still trying to figure that out, Mick. If you guys can positively I.D. him as the guy you saw at the landing, I can go to the cops and solve a big-assed piece of this puzzle."

They continued to stare at the picture. It was dark that night, and there were a lot of shadows, and the guy's face was now bruised and bloodied. I knew it would be tough, but it was a shot. Just then, Mickey took the picture in his right hand, and covered everything but the eyes with his left. I watched as he showed it to Herbie, who stared at it wide eyed. He looked at Mickey and nodded. Handing me the picture, Mickey nodded at me and said, "That's him."

"You're sure?" I asked them.

"Yeah," said Herbie. "They was wearin' masks, you know, and all we could see was their eyes at first."

"Same bastard messed up Casey, too," Mickey said, with a growing anger in his voice.

I trusted these guys and their memories. They would know a stranger on their turf, and they would remember if they saw him again. I was equally sure that if this was the guy who put a beating on his friend, Mickey would definitely know. I suggested we go up and see Casey, and all three of us went into the hospital together. Once inside, the volunteer at the reception desk informed us that his condition had deteriorated to poor. We took the elevator to the ICU.

At the ICU, I identified myself to the nurse. She was the same one I spoke to the other day when Casey was brought in. She informed me that his kidneys were failing, and so was his liver from all of the internal injuries from the beating. She explained there were new tubes in his chest to re-inflate his lungs, which collapsed from the multiple fractures of his ribcage, and the doctor was called in to drain fluid from around his heart. Herbie and Mickey went in to

LAKE EFFECT

visit with their friend, and I waited outside the room. I was thinking about Victor, and what the next step should be. I would need to find out who put him on Lawrence, and me, and if there were more like Victor out there. I thought for a minute about what would send a upper class white kid, who was studying to be a lawyer, into the bad guy business, but I quickly came to the realization that was for sociologists and social workers to figure out, not guys like me. I looked down the hall and noticed a payphone at the end, so I figured I'd try to call Paula at her cousin's house and make sure they were settled in.

I dug a quarter out of my pocket and dropped it in the slot. I dialed and the line was busy, so I decided to try again later. I stepped back into the doorway of Casey's room and watched as Herbie and Mickey kept a quiet stream of conversation going, speaking with their fallen friend as if it were just another day at the pier. I had to admire the way these men stuck together, and were there for each other. I don't know many people like that, and don't know many people who know people like that. In a world of hurt and mean they were their own oasis. I walked in softly, not wanting to interrupt the vigil, paid my respects, and left them to each other.

Out in the cold parking lot my cell phone rang. It was Jimmy Ramone.

"Joe, I got something interesting for you," he said.

"Geez, you guys work pretty quick when you get a little detective competition," I teased.

"Listen, smart ass, I'm trying to help you out. You want it or not?"

"Sorry, Jimmy, it's too cold out here to pick at each other. What do you have?"

"Toxicology report came in on the Dellaplante kids. Found high levels of a drug called amytriptiline, commonly called Elavil, in both kids."

I had heard of Elavil. It was a mood elevator sometimes prescribed for depression to help the patients sleep. Somebody knew what they were doing, and didn't want the children to suffer. That thought

107

chilled me more than the weather. "Anything else, Jim?" I asked nervously.

"Actually, there is. Wanna take a guess what we found in the glove box of the mini-van?" he asked back.

"A prescription bottle for Elavil with Sharon Dellaplante's name on it."

"Good guess," he said. "You might be okay at this detective shit after all. Doesn't look good for her."

"No, it doesn't," I replied. "Could be a set-up?"

"Could be. You've talked to her already. Is that what you think?"

"What I think is I need to find out more about what's going on before I start thinking. Victor make bail yet?"

"Maybe 15 or 20 minutes after you left. Did you know Victor's daddy and mommy are both attorneys?"

"The family that sues together…," I said.

"Indeed. What are you going to do about Sharon Dellaplante?" Jimmy asked.

"I was thinking it depends on what the Hamburg PD was planning on doing. You guys gonna bring her in?"

"Was thinking about it, but she might cooperate with you more readily than with us at this point. Besides, we're still working out details with the Sheriff's Department as to who gets bragging rights on this one."

"I had nothing better planned today. I'll be in touch."

I no sooner hung up with Jimmy Ramone then the phone rang again. This time it was Paula, a much better surprise.

"Hey there," I said, smiling. "I tried to call you earlier but the line was busy."

"Sorry, but I decided to help you out a little so I went online," she told me. "I want my house and my husband back as soon as possible."

"I can appreciate that. It is gonna be really quiet tonight without you and the kids. What were you looking for, Paula?"

"You mentioned a company, NPA Productions, and that they were an offshore gambling site. So I decided to take a look around. I hope you don't mind."

LAKE EFFECT

"Nope. I can use all the help I can get," I told her. "What did you come up with?"

"Well, nothing special really. I mean it is set up for taking online bets on anything, and I do mean anything. Baseball, basketball, football, side bets, casino gambling, you name it. You can even lay a bet on the next field of democratic presidential nominees."

"That's great, hon, but it is all pretty much what I would have expected."

"And one more thing… did you know they post a deadbeat list?" she asked, with a tone of voice that seemed to say 'gotcha'.

"Don't tell me, let me guess, our favorite real estate developer is on the list?" I asked, admiring her sense of fun.

"Yup, you bet. And so is Michael Lawrence, believe it or not."

"Really," I said. "That is a surprise."

"Thought so. Impressed?"

"Always. How are the kids, and you?"

"We're okay. Carrie was up and getting breakfast early, trying to make things as normal as she can. But it's not normal to wake up here. It's not normal to have to live out of a suitcase while my husband works around bad guys and dead guys. Kyle wants to know if we get to go home when Daddy catches the bad guys. So do I."

I am sure there have been times that I have felt more anger and sadness, but none came to mind. I hated when the job interfered with my family. You learn to live with it, never to like it. "Yeah," I grunted. "Soon."

"I hope so. We miss you already. Be careful, Joe, please?"

"Absolutely. And I'll call you later tonight. Love you."

"You better," Paula said, then hung up.

I got back in the car, and started back to the office. I stopped to pick up some coffee and bagels on the way, figuring Sam would appreciate a late morning snack before lunchtime. She did, and I filled her in on the latest and greatest in the world of crime fighting over hot coffee, French vanilla cappuccino, and bagels and cream cheese. Sam asked how the kids and Paula were, and told me if I needed her to help out she would be more than happy to. She was a good friend, and was genuinely concerned. I told her where they were staying, just in case of anything. After eating, I decided to call ahead to Sharon Dellaplante, intending to get there this afternoon. A woman answered the phone, but it didn't sound like Sharon.

"Hello?" she said hoarsely.

"Hello, may I speak to Sharon, please?" I asked, as professionally as I knew how.

"No. Who's calling?" the woman asked.

"This is Joe Banks. Whom am I speaking to, please?"

"Jesus, Banks," the voice on the other line croaked. "This is Maddy, her sister. Don't you know when to leave well enough alone?"

"Maddy, you sound like hell. Are you alright?" I asked, actually caring whether or not she was. I may have my problems with the old man, but I was beginning to feel for the daughters.

"No, I'm not. I feel truly crappy, and you aren't helping at all. What do you want with Shar?"

"There is some new information I need to discuss with her, but you could help me a lot. Was she being treated for depression, or any other anxiety disorder?"

"You're serious, aren't you?" she asked. I heard a long exhale on the other end of the line.

"Very. I need to know what's going on and this may be a piece of the puzzle."

Another long exhale. I think she may have been smoking, which goes a long way towards explaining the hoarseness in her voice. "She was having trouble raising the two kids by herself, she told everyone. Daddy saw she was losing weight, had really dark circles under her eyes, and said she felt tired and hadn't been sleeping at all. So he took her to see his doctor and he gave her a prescription to help her sleep."

"Do you know the name of the pills she was taking?"

"Yeah, Elavil. I thought she should probably be on Prozac or something like that, but the doctor told her she needed to relax enough to sleep, and that would make life more manageable."

"How long ago was this? It's important."

LAKE EFFECT

"Back around Thanksgiving, I think. You know how freaked out some people get around the holidays."

"Thanks, Maddy. This is a big help. Now where did you say your sister is?" I asked.

"She staying with Daddy for a few days. He thought it would be best until she feels better," she said, her voice clearing somewhat.

"So I can reach her there?"

"You can try, I guess."

"Thanks, again. Take care of yourself." I hung up the phone and took a long drink from my coffee cup. I didn't like the way Maddy Dellaplante sounded, and I wasn't sure I liked the fact that Sharon moved back in with her father. Perhaps there had been a thaw in their relationship since the death of her two children, but she seemed to me to be more mentally tough than her sister would lead me to believe.

"Sharon's not there?" Sam asked.

"Nope," I replied. "Moved back home with Daddy Dellaplante for a few days, according to Maddy."

"Really? That's a surprise, given what you've told me about her and 'Daddy Dearest'."

"Yeah, surprised me, too."

"Do you think he'll let you talk to her?" Sam asked between sips of her cappuccino.

"Won't really know until I ask, but he'll want to be there if he does."

"Have you told Lawrence about catching the guy who was stalking him?"

"Not yet," I told her, throwing my empty cup into the trashcan, basketball style for three points. "After I talk to Sharon."

"Do you think she gave the drugs to the kids?"

"Jimmy Ramone thinks so, and if Kevin Garner knows, he'll think so too. As for me, I'll keep an open mind until I talk to her myself."

I watched Sam finish her bagel and coffee, walk politely over to the trash can to throw her things out, and as she turned back to my desk, she asked, "So what do you want to do about lunch?"

RONALD W. ADAMS

All I could do was shake my head.

Seventeen

I was able to get through to Frank Dellaplante and convince him of the need to speak to Sharon. After the obligatory bluster and threats, Frank finally agreed to let me meet with her at his house in the morning. I had also tried unsuccessfully to reach Michael Lawrence, so I had had my quota of frustration for one day. Between last night and this morning I was feeling the need to work off a little pent-up aggression, so I decided to hit the gym on the way back to the house. It wasn't like there was going to be anyone waiting for me tonight.

I don't concentrate on one body area per work-out, like some of the local fitness gurus recommend. I prefer a long, slow, sustained, overall workout with all of the sweat and none of the style points some people seem to favor these days. The gym I work out at near the house started several years back as a 'weight closet', a place for hardcore power lifters and bodybuilders. Now they feature spinning classes, Tae Bo classes, and daycare for the suburban mom, trying to stop her own personal suburban sprawl. As for myself, I tend to stay to myself, angry at the world and everything in it when I work out. It keeps mindless banter to a minimum and concentration to a maximum. Like I said, it is a release for all the things I can't do with and to the bad guys.

My workout lasted about an hour and a half, including treadmill work. I love the feeling of the muscle tension you get with a hard workout. It makes you want to bite the head off something just because you can. I indulged myself in one of the protein shakes the club makes for all its upper class clientele. As I finished it, I thought to myself it was probably better for me than a fast food burger, but wouldn't taste as good with a beer. The kid behind the shake bar looked to be half my age, roughly, and judging from his physique hadn't even seen a picture of a beer. I decided excess, even in health, was not good for anyone.

When I got home, I checked for messages. There were two from credit card companies reminding me I was late with a payment. Those were deleted quickly. I threw my gym bag full of sweat-soaked clothes to the bottom of the basement stairs, when the front doorbell rang. At first I reached for my gun, and felt almost instantly stupid as I realized that anyone who wanted to hurt me or my family would probably not be polite enough to ring the bell. I looked to the glass panels beside the front door, and there was Kevin Garner, bearing beer. He smiled, raised the six pack of Sam Adams into view, and I unlocked the door.

"Sam at your office told me you were a self-imposed bachelor tonight, so I thought some beer and a hockey game would be in order," he said, handing me a bottle on his way to my fridge.

"C'mon in, make yourself at home," I told him sarcastically, twisting the cap off the beer. "I'm just getting in from the gym and was feeling way too healthy, anyway."

Kevin dumped the beer in the refrigerator and his coat over one of the high back kitchen chairs. He passed through to the family room, found the remote control and turned on the Sabres game. "Great, 'cuz I called and ordered a pizza for delivery on my way over."

"The last time I had a pizza you ordered was that crazy Cajun chicken pizza with jalapenos that burned the hair off my feet," I told him, the memory of that episode of heartburn still fresh. I grabbed a bag of corn tortilla chips out of the pantry on the way through the kitchen. I walked in to the family room and flopped on the couch, which is such a guy thing to do that I rarely do it when Paula and the kids are home. I opened the bag and grabbed a few chips.

"So what have you found out?" Kevin asked, and then took a long slug off his beer. I twisted the top off mine, and drained about a third of it. It tasted much better than the protein shake I had at the gym.

"Well, to catch you up," I started, "I found out somebody had the kids murdered, and chances are they never felt a thing because they were drugged. I found out that some of the parties connected to all this are holding out on me, and whatever they are holding out got my house broken into, and got my wife and kids scared enough to move

LAKE EFFECT

out. I found out the same genius who is smart enough to be admitted to U.B. for pre-law wasn't bright enough to avoid wearing the same jacket while stalking Lawrence and breaking into my home." I paused, took another hit off my beer bottle, and then continued. "And most interesting of all, I have two witnesses that believe that this same genius was at the landing the night the Dellaplante kids died."

"Sounds like progress," he replied, staring at the action on the television. "Sounds like you are hot on the trail." He reached into the bag and pulled out a fistful of chips.

"Yeah but I keep getting as many questions as answers. For instance, did you know that Sharon Dellaplante was taking the same medication they found in the kids' bloodstream during the autopsy?" I asked him.

"What medication was that?" he asked, swallowing.

"Elavil, it's used for depression. Frank Dellaplante ever talk to you about his kid having problems?"

"Nope, but to be honest, Frank isn't actually the caring, sharing type. Or haven't you noticed?" he asked sarcastically.

"Oh yeah, I've noticed," I said, with the game getting intense in the background. I took another drink from my bottle, watching yet another acrobatic save by Hasek. Even on the downside of his career, he can still make a spectacular move to completely stymie the best goal scorers.

"How's the guy from the lake doing? He still at Mercy?" Kevin asked, not moving his eyes from the screen.

"Yeah, he's still pretty bad. I think I know who put him there, but I'm gonna have to go outside the lines a little. All these things are connected, and they all seem to keep pointing at either of the Dellaplantes, father or daughter."

"What about the Lawrence kid?"

"Possible, but not likely. Too much trouble to put a tail on yourself if all you want to do is throw the cops off. I think I need to get the kid I caught in the house to open up just a little bit."

Just then the doorbell rang. It was the local pizza delivery guy, with tonight's heartburn du jour. As he stood in the doorway, I could

RONALD W. ADAMS

smell the onions, pepperoni and hot peppers on the rising steam from the box. I called to Kevin, "It's for you."

Kevin came to the door, paid the guy and took the pizza in to the family room. As a concession to the civilization marriage and family brings to the barely housebroken male, I grabbed some paper plates, napkins, and two fresh beers, and followed him in. I also checked for antacid, just in case. I had a feeling I was in for a long night.

Eighteen

Kevin left about midnight, shortly after the Sabres fought to yet another brilliant 1-1 tie with Toronto. His pizza unfortunately, hung around a lot longer. I finally closed my eyes about 2 am, and was rudely awakened by the sound of the ringing telephone at about 6:30 am.

"Banks," I croaked into the phone.

"Jesus, what's up? Your wife and kids aren't home one night and you go out on a bender?" the voice on the other end chided.

"It was a bad combination of a well-meaning friend and a hostile pizza. It got ugly, I don't want to talk about it."

"It's Ramone. We're putting out a warrant on your best buddy, Victor Maloney. It seems your pal, Casey from the boat launch, didn't make it. He died about two hours ago," Jimmy said. "Sorry that had to be the first thing you heard this morning, but I figure you might have an idea on how to get to this kid before we do. It might make things easier if you could encourage his next visit to be voluntary."

"You got his home address, you go get him," I groaned as I pushed myself up to sit on the edge of the bed.

"I'm surprised, Joe. I thought you'd be dying for another piece of him."

"That's not why you want me to get him. You can't find him, can you?"

There was a long silence on the other end of the line. Lack of sleep put me in a bad mood, and Ramone was going to catch the first of it. "Jim, tell me you didn't lose a murder suspect, one who may a be suspect in a total of three murders. Tell me."

"Just get him, Joe," Jim pleaded. "You know what he looks like, you know where he might go, and you are the best guy for the job."

"You're lucky I'm up to my ass in this case as it is. Now I have to see it through, for my own piece of mind. But you have got to promise me that there's more information coming from forensics. I need to settle this thing."

"Bring Maloney in to me, and I will give you whatever you need," Ramone replied. "Buffalo Police went to his house around five this morning, and he wasn't there. His parents claim he hadn't been home all night."

Ramone gave me the address, which was in the Delaware Park area. I worked my way out of bed and down to the kitchen. Every move reminded me of how hard I worked out last night, and the muscles in my thighs rebelled at going down stairs. I put on the coffee, and walked back upstairs to the shower. I thought to myself six freaking thirty in the morning and it's already gonna be a long day. The hot water started waking me up, and by the time I let it beat on my aching neck and back, almost half an hour passed and I was feeling much more human. I put my coffee in the insulated stainless steel travel mug Paula bought me several Christmases ago. I freaked about how much she paid for it at the time, but I appreciate it now.

On the way to Victor Maloney's house, around eight o'clock, I called the office and spoke to Sam, whom I was lucky enough to catch in early. I asked her to follow up with Sharon Dellaplante. I told her to call Frank Dellaplante's home number, which I had in the Rolodex on my desk. Once that was done, I called Paula to check on her and the kids. Assured everybody got through the night okay, and that the big plans for the day included building a snowman, I was able to get focused on finding Victor. I got off the I-190 and on to the Scajaquada Expressway, and headed for the Nottingham Terrace address Jimmy Ramone gave me. Traffic was starting to fill in, so it took me a few extra minutes to get there. Thankfully, Buffalo remains the 20-minute city, because back in Boston it would be a good hour just to go the 16 miles from my house to the Maloney's.

I knew I had the right place because the car that I saw parked outside my house the other night after the ambulance picked up Victor from my kitchen floor, and the one I saw with Michael Lawrence when I first discovered Victor's talent as a hired hand, was sitting in the driveway, covered in salt from the wheel wells to the windows. I looked through the windows hoping to see something that might be useful. It looked like the inside of a college kid's car, with scattered

LAKE EFFECT

binders, law review journals, and a sociology textbook. There was also a notepad, with some telephone numbers scratched on it. I reached into the top inside pocket of my coat and took out a post-it pad and pencil, copying the numbers I could read to check out later. Maybe I would have either Paula or Sam call a couple, just to see what turns up.

I was just finishing writing the last number down, and was in the process of putting the notepad away when from behind me I heard the sound of crunching snow as someone was approaching. I turned to see a middle aged man, with a corona of white hair, a gray mohair overcoat and navy blue striped pajama bottoms tucked into a pair of duck boots. I recognized some of the same features as Victor Maloney, so I assumed this guy to be his father. His expression was grim, humorless, and entirely unwelcoming.

"Why are you trespassing at my house?" he asked quickly and angrily.

"I am looking for Victor, Mr. Maloney. My name is Banks, I'm a private investigator," I called to him.

"He's not here, Banks. I've already had the police here early this morning, what do you want with him?"

"Same thing I expect. Where is your son, Mr. Maloney?" I watched his shoulder slouch just a little, and I could tell by the way he was shifting his weight, swaying from side to side, that he was getting cold. "You know he is wanted in connection with the death of Casimir Kasparczak?"

"The police told me," he said matter of factly.

"It would be easier if I find him first, sir."

"You think you can? Find him, that is," Maloney asked, his eyes hopeful.

"It is what I do. You don't know where he is, or you won't say?"

"No, Mr. Banks, I don't know where he is. As an attorney, I would advise him not to go in with either you or the police until I spoke with him first. But he hasn't been home all night or all day yesterday. We, his mother and I, expected him home after classes. He usually calls if he is going to be late. He had been a little evasive

119

as to what he was up to lately, and to come home the other morning with his face all beaten as it was, it really upset us both. He was home long enough to change his clothes and he went back out, to school I suppose. I never knew him to be in any kind of trouble, but now…" He shook his head and looked down at his boots.

"Mr. Maloney, can you give me an idea if there are any friends that he hangs out with, anyone else who would know where Victor might have gone?" I asked.

Maloney thought for a minute. "He has been spending a lot of time with this guy from Derby, a fellow by the name of Lawrence, Michael Lawrence I think he said. But I know he has a part-time job that he has been working also. He told us that he got hurt on the job, that was why his face was so badly bruised."

"Did he say what his part-time job was, Mr. Maloney?" I asked him, not wanting to let him know what his son was doing that got him hurt.

"He said he was working for campus security at school. He told me he got hurt breaking up a fight on campus. You are going to look for him, aren't you? It is what you do, you said."

"Yes it is."

"Do you know what the police want with him, Mr. Banks? Did he kill that man?"

"He played a role. Beyond that, I need to find him to know what the role was." Maybe I should have told him, but one father to another, I wasn't ready to tell him his son may have been involved in three murders.

Maloney nodded. He turned back to his house, his head down, the snow making a crunching, squeaking sound as he walked.

I got back in my car and started back toward the Dellaplante Development truck yard. If Michael Lawrence knew this kid, I wanted to know why he neglected to inform me of this little tidbit. I called Sam on my cell phone and gave her the telephone numbers I got from Victor's car and asked her to call them and check them out. I told her that I was going to talk to Michael Lawrence, and that I'd check back in later. I then called Garner at his office.

LAKE EFFECT

"Investigations, Garner," he said.

"Kevin, it's Joe," I said. "Busy?"

"Naw, nothing that won't keep. What's up?"

"You still friendly with the Dellaplantes?"

"Right now, I would describe it as courteous, not so much friendly. Why, what are you getting at, Joe?"

"Might not be anything, but remember I told you about the guy who was following Mike Lawrence, and wound up breaking in to my house? It turns out they know each other, Kev. Sound right to you?"

"What's the connection?"

"One of the guys from the landing, one of the witnesses to the van being dumped died of his injuries last night. This kid, Maloney, the same kid I was telling you about, was positively identified as the attacker. Now he goes missing, and the father tells me he might be visiting Lawrence."

"Not good," Kevin sighed.

"No. Do me a favor, call and talk to Sharon Dellaplante. I don't care what you talk about. Just make sure she's okay, and tell her I will be in touch soon."

"I can do that. You want me to call you and let you know?"

"Yeah, please do. I'm on my way to Dellaplante's yard to see about Michael Lawrence. I'll keep you posted," I told him.

"Great. By the way, I authorized another check to you, and to pay on the kid's policies to Sharon Dellaplante."

"Thanks, I'll be in touch." I hung up and put the phone on the passenger seat.

If Lawrence was more involved than he was letting on, how was he connected? It bothered me that he would act like the Maloney kid was stalking him. I was turning on to Route 400 heading south, and I decided to act on a hunch. I called Jimmy Ramone and told him that good old Victor was now among the missing, and that I was on my way to the Dellaplante Development office to see Michael Lawrence.

121

Nineteen

In a maintenance garage in the back of the truck yard, Michael Lawrence paced back and forth. A lit cigarette sloped from his mouth, the smoke mixing with the condensation from his breath as he stomped his feet against the cold. He wore a charcoal wool trench coat over his suit and tie, with only a pair of black wingtips on his feet. He was not dressed to be outdoors for long, and the more he paced, the more he hated it. He pulled down the wristband of his black leather glove on his left hand, staring at his watch. It was 7:30am. He looked out of the entrance door, which stood besides the huge overhead door, and cursed the cold under his breath. Even with the doors shut this place is cold as hell, he thought to himself. The smell of diesel and gasoline fumes hung in the air, and stung his nose as much as the frigid air.

Lawrence checked his watch again. Seven thirty five. Christ, he thought, I have to calm down, be patient. Walking back towards the tool crib, he heard the door opening. He turned as Frank Dellaplante entered the garage, wearing a brown Carhart work coat over a heavy Eddie Bauer flannel shirt, sweatshirt, and jeans. His insulated work shoes made almost no noise as he walked across the concrete floor, the occasional piles of Speedi-Dri having long ago soaked up their designated puddles. On his hands were a pair of Thinsulated leather gloves, further testament to the fact that he was used to working in these conditions, more so than Lawrence. Dellaplante was a builder, who worked his way up to the top. Lawrence was a business school graduate whose parents put him through college. To the casual observer, it would have been difficult to tell who was the employer and who was the employee.

"Lawrence," Dellaplante called. "What are you doing out here?"

"Just catching a smoke," Lawrence responded, tossing the remains of his cigarette on to the floor. He looked down at the butt as he ground it out with his toe. "Were you looking for me, sir?"

"Yes, Cyndi said you were out here. I just got off the phone with my daughter Maddy."

"Is everything alright?" Lawrence asked, shifting his stance from left to right and back again in a vain attempt to ward off the cold.

"Fine. She was asking for you, Michael."

"Oh? Did she leave a message or anything?"

"No. Do you know what she wanted with you?" the older man asked, his annoyance growing.

"How would I know, sir? I was out here, I didn't even know she called until you told me."

Dellaplante stared at Lawrence for a moment. Then he turned back towards the door, speaking loudly as he left, "One daughter's life is ruined, don't start with the other one. Do I make myself clear?"

"Yes, sir. Crystal," Lawrence replied, smiling behind the old man's back. He looked down at his watch again. He was getting more anxious. Screw it, he thought to himself, as he walked towards the door to head back inside where it had to be warmer.

Lawrence stepped carefully as he walked across the construction yard towards his office. It was a trick to balance on the slick snow and mud, but he managed to safely traverse the yard without any major damage to his suit or shoes. As he pulled the door open, he noticed a man leaning forward on his hands at the receptionist's desk. Lawrence took off his jacket and gloves, stamping his feet to generate a little circulation. Cyndi should know better, he thought to himself. "Cyndi, I don't think this is the time or the place for..." he started.

The man straightened up, and turned to face Lawrence. "She's alright," Victor Maloney said, smiling under his bandaged nose. "In more ways than one."

Cyndi smiled back at him, and chirped, "Mikey, umm, Mr. Lawrence, this gentleman is here to see you."

Lawrence glared at Maloney for an instant, then said to his receptionist, "Fine. Just give me a minute, please."

Lawrence strode slowly into his office and closed the door abruptly. He stuffed his gloves into the pockets of his coat, and hung the coat on a tree behind his door. He moved to his desk and sat down; reaching into the lower right hand drawer for the .22 caliber semi-automatic pistol he kept there. Lawrence closed the drawer,

LAKE EFFECT

and pressed the intercom button on the telephone. "Cyndi, you can show Mr. Maloney in now," he said.

Twenty

It was almost nine o'clock by the time I reached the Dellaplante Development truck yard. The Jeep sloshed and slogged through the half frozen mud from the salt-thawed snow in the parking lot. Through the entrance doors, I could see my old pal Cyndi with the 'Y' and the 'I' reversed. I kicked the snow off my boots and walked in to a fresh-faced smile, with just a hint of face recognition.

"You're Mikey's friend Joe, right?" she smiled.

"Yup, that's me," I replied, smiling back. I wondered if this girl ever not smiled, but her world was probably a happy little place.

"Aw, you just missed him by about ten minutes. He left with another guy, a Vic something or other, going for coffee or something like that he said."

That was interesting. "Jeez, and that was my idea today, too. Did he say when he'd be back, Cyndi?"

"Naw, he didn't. Sorry."

Just then, the phone on her desk buzzed. She answered it with her normal cheerfulness, which slowly disappeared through the call. She never said a word after hello until she finally looked at me and said, "Mr. Dellaplante wants to see you in his office. Last door on the right."

I thanked her and proceeded down the short painted concrete hall. There were plaques commemorating championship little league baseball, football, and hockey teams, all sponsored by Dellaplante Development. There was a water fountain halfway down the hall, so I took advantage before going in to see Dellaplante. I reached the end of the hall and knocked confidently on the door. Obviously overwhelmed by my application of knuckle to wood, there was no response, so I opened the door and walked in.

Dellaplante's office was much more austere than I imagined it would be. I guessed it would be more grandiose, more over the top. Instead it looked like a project engineer's office, with pictures and artist's renderings of the most recent projects on the unadorned walls and a large drafting table cluttered with blueprints in one corner. A simple metal desk was found in the back of the office, with Dellaplante hunched over a stack of papers. "I didn't know you were coming here today," he said sharply, looking up from his pile.

"I didn't either, yet here I am. I didn't know you knew I was here," I told him.

"I make it my business to know what goes on around here. If you weren't here to see me or to flirt with my genius secretary, I can assume then you were here to see Lawrence?" he asked.

"I was, but it seems I missed him just now. Do you know where he went or when he'll be back?"

"No, I don't. The last I saw of him was out in the equipment barn, having a smoke. You know it amazes me that someone could be that weak to be addicted to a habit that could kill you, and force you to be uncomfortably cold in the middle of winter just to participate. If there is a habit that makes you miserable, why bother..."

I cleared my throat, and he stopped abruptly, looking at me as if I had just reminded him of his own self-destructive habits. He cut the sermon short, and I was once again safe from the world according to Frank.

"Weren't you supposed to see Sharon this morning, Mr. Banks?" he asked me, looking at his watch.

"I had Kevin Garner call her to tell her I wasn't going to be able to make it. Something more immediate came up, but I still want to talk to her. Is she still at your home, or is she back at her place?"

Dellaplante thought for a moment, then answered, "I think Maddy was going to take her back to her hovel in Derby this morning, and stay with her a little while. You can probably get her there later this morning."

I thanked him for his time and extended my hand, telling him I would be in touch. He quickly said, "You know, I haven't received a bill for your services yet."

"You will," I replied, smiling.

I passed Cyndi's desk and asked if Lawrence was back from his coffee session with Vic Something. She chuckled and said he wasn't.

"I'll tell you what, how about if I leave a note for him." I reached

LAKE EFFECT

into my coat pocket for a small spiral notepad and pen and scribbled a quick note. Handing it to Cyndi, I folded it and said, "Please make sure you give this to Mike as soon as he gets through the door, okay? And remind him to call me, please. He gets so busy he may forget."

Cyndi's slender fingers took the note from my hand, and she looked at me for a second. Then she asked, "Joe, do you mind if I ask what company you work for? I mean, you seem to be able to go where you want during the day, go out for coffee with friends, whatever. Sounds like a great job to me."

I thought about it for a minute, then replied, "Well, to be honest, I work for myself. The hours stink, and the pay is lousy, but I do love my boss. And as a fringe benefit, I get to sleep with his wife almost anytime I want to."

That sent her into a little giggling fit, and I took the opportunity to get out of there. I drove to the nearest coffee and donut shop to grab some breakfast, and to take stock of the day's events. Here I was with a lot of loose ends and only a vague idea of what ties them together. I hate that feeling. I went through the drive-thru line, placed my order, got my coffee and apple fritter, and headed back towards the office. I was hoping to finish my breakfast before encountering the human eating machine that is my secretary Sam.

My cell phone rang on the passenger seat, so I grabbed it, and answered with my usual curt response. And, as usual, it was Paula reminding me how customer unfriendly I sound.

"Having a good morning?" she asked.

"Not really, about like always when the bad guys separate me from my wife and kids and confuse the hell out of me by basically acting like bad guys," I replied. "How are things with you?"

"The kids miss you, and I haven't had to yell at anyone to pick up their underwear from the bathroom floor. It evens out."

"I have to check the mail when I get home, I think there's something from Garner in there today."

"Good," Paula said with a little sigh. She always preferred when the cash flowed in the right direction. "So what's the latest on our little burglar?"

129

RONALD W. ADAMS

"Well, as predicted, he made bail on the assumption he was not a flight risk. Bad assumption, so he is out and about somewhere. And, as it turns out, he has graduated from burglary to murder. One of the guys from the lake died last night, the one he allegedly beat the shit out of. And just to make things a little more interesting, Casey's friends identified him as one of the assholes they saw the night of the murder of the Dellaplante kids."

"So, when do we get to come home?" Paula asked hopefully. "Carrie's house is nice, but it's a little cramped for three adults, four kids and assorted pets."

"I'm sure. But I want to find out where this Maloney guy is before I think it's safe for you to come home. You understand?"

"I understand, but I don't have to like it."

"It's not mandatory, but look at the bright side. I'm not the one to blame for messes for a while."

"I know," she said sarcastically, "but how bad are you trashing MY house?"

"Just think bulldozer, and you'll feel better," I told her.

"Of course."

130

Twenty-One

Maddy Dellaplante turned her Range Rover down the slick, poorly plowed side street that led to her sister Sharon's trailer. Sharon slept in the passenger seat beside her, a combination of physical and emotional exhaustion overtaking her with the help of her anti-depressant medication. Maddy silently shook her head as she approached the trailer, as she did every time she went there. No matter how many times her father offered to help her, Sharon was always looking to make her own way. And that was why she was Daddy's favorite. That thought alone was enough to infuriate the older daughter.

When daddy wanted her to go to piano lessons, Maddy studied harder than anyone in her class. Sharon decided she would rather play softball, and tag with the boys in the neighborhood. When it was dancing lessons, Maddy was the lead performer at almost every recital. Sharon couldn't care less about what was expected of her, and sought new and exciting ways to frustrate and confound her well-to-do, society pillar parents. That her parents tolerated it, and her father seemingly encouraged it, made no sense, Maddy thought. And when Maddy pursued a business degree and finally an MBA in management from her father's alma mater, Sharon opted to get pregnant, stay unmarried, and eventually work for minimum wage in a job provided for her through family connections. Sharon was always the prodigal daughter, and Maddy always held her in high contempt for constantly falling in shit and always coming out smelling like a rose.

Maddy pulled in the driveway, and stepped into the ankle deep snow that had fallen since they were there last. She slipped slightly as she rounded the front of her SUV to help her groggy sister in to the house. Sharon grunted as Maddy pulled the passenger door open and a frozen breeze hit her face. Maddy took her hand, fairly pulling her out of the vehicle, and held her tightly to keep her from falling. How many times had she performed this very favor for Sharon when she came home from a high school football game drunk, usually

131

with an erotic bruise on the side of her neck. She leaned her sister against the steel siding of the trailer long enough to open the door, then she guided Sharon through it. Maddy then unceremoniously dumped her into the nearest dinette chair with a thud.

She took her own snow-covered boots off, and then turned her attention to her sister slumped to one side. She untied and pulled each boot off, then as an afterthought, stood Sharon up and walked her through the puddle of melted snow that formed at her feet. That brought a secret smile to Maddy's face, like the mean kid in class who snaps the back of your ear in the middle of the lecture. The two women trudged down the narrow hallway, bouncing from wall to wall, until they reached Sharon's bedroom. Maddy sat her down, turned down her comforter, and laid her down to sleep.

Maddy closed the door to the bedroom and went to the living room to turn on the television. Of course, she thought to herself, no cable. How did this girl live? She looked around, everywhere the remainders of a household full of toys and childhood. Over on the coffee table was a newsprint tablet full of crayon scribbles, and stacks of blocks and piles of beads in the corners of the room. David's trucks were lined up in a makeshift parking lot behind the loveseat, and Sarah's dolls were sitting in a silent tea party at a small picnic table near the kitchen. To someone who wasn't used to the sight, it appeared as unkempt. Maddy regarded the view as a disheveled mess, and began putting the toys away in a toy box, perhaps to give away to Goodwill or the Salvation Army. As she worked, she put on the television noon news as background noise.

She worked steadily until finally all the toys were boxed up and put away. Maddy muttered to herself as to why Sharon ever let the house get that cluttered. Certainly she would never allow her children to get away with that. It was about mid afternoon, while Sharon continued to snore softly in her bedroom, when the black Chevy pickup truck pulled into the driveway. Maddy went to the kitchen door and opened it, waiting. A man in a dark overcoat got out of the truck and shuffled through the snow to the woman waiting by the door. They embraced, sharing a passionate kiss by the open door.

LAKE EFFECT

"Hi honey, I'm home," teased Lawrence.

"Mmmm, I'm glad you are, lover," purred Maddy.

"And I remembered to make a stop on the way from work," he said, tossing a pharmacy bag on the kitchen table.

Twenty-two

Sam sat at her desk, her hair pulled back into a loose ponytail, and a yellow number 2 pencil stuck flirtatiously behind her right ear. The uniform of the day, since we weren't expecting any company, consisted of a pair of black high-heeled boots, dark blue jeans, and a gray St. Bonaventure sweatshirt. And, as usual, there was a king sized coffee mug and a half eaten bagel on the corner of her desk. I came into the room just as she was hanging up the phone.

"Little early for pizza delivery, isn't it?" I said, taking my coat off.

"I do other things besides you eat, you know," she said.

"So you keep saying."

"I am more than just a pretty face with an appetite. I am an investigative assistant," she announced.

"So assist me," I said, sitting down behind my desk. I reached for my business card file box and Rolodex.

"I called the number you gave me," Sam started, leaning against the end of my desk. "And as it turns out, I got Michael Lawrence's voice mail."

"I figured as much. I went out to see Lawrence at Dellaplante Development, and missed him. It seems he went out for coffee with our boy Maloney."

"Hmmm, so what do you think, boss?"

"I'm thinking maybe our dear Mr. Lawrence isn't squeaky clean after all. I've got to find him and Maloney now."

"Oh yeah, by the way," Sam shot in, "Paula called just a little while ago."

"Yeah? Something up?" I asked. I spoke to her a short time ago and she didn't mention anything, so it got me a little curious.

"Just checking to make sure you're telling her everything," Sam said.

"What makes her think checking with you insures I'm telling her everything?"

Sam gave me the same look Paula gives me when I ask her a

135

stupid question. Come to think of it, Amanda has the same look. It must be a gene that only women have. I shook my head in surrender.

The phone rang, and there was a brief non-verbal power struggle to see who would answer it. After three rings, Sam picked up the phone and, just before answering, stuck her tongue out at me. It's good to be the boss sometimes. "Banks Investigations," I heard her answer. "Just a minute, Kevin." She handed the phone to me.

"Yeah," I said, watching Sam do her victory strut across the office.

"Joe, I haven't been able to get a hold of Sharon Dellaplante," Kevin explained.

"I spoke to old man Dellaplante a little while ago, said her sister Maddy was taking her back to her house again."

"I know, so I've been trying to call her house, you know, follow up for you and for me. So far all I've gotten is Maddy and a promise Sharon would call as soon as she gets in."

"Uh-oh," I said, knowing I could always be counted on for my profundity.

"Big uh-oh, pal," Kevin said. "I don't like it at all."

"Nope. Wanna meet there or here?"

"There. See you in about 45 minutes," he said hanging up.

I told Sam what was up, and grabbed my coat off the rack. I asked her to keep calling every few minutes to try to reach Sharon Dellaplante. With any luck besides bad I would be at her house in about 30 minutes. I was beginning to get a little nervous.

"And please, please, call Paula and tell her I'm okay. I'll call her later on, and tell her I'll see her tonight," I said.

"No more need for the 'safe house' thing at Carrie's?" Sam asked, already picking up the phone.

"I don't think so, but I'll talk to her about it later when I get there."

I got to the Jeep and slipped it into 4-wheel drive to accommodate the heavy, wet snow that was beginning to coat the roads. I cruised through the village, and headed down Route 5 towards Derby. I could tell by the way the wind was coming in off the lake we were in for one of the area's notorious 'lake effect' snowstorms. When the

LAKE EFFECT

air coming over the lake is colder than the lake temperature, the moisture it picks up from the water gets converted to snow and summarily dumped on us. Sometimes it was an inch or two at a time, other times it might be a foot or more, and even the weatherman can't be sure. The flakes coming down were big and fluffy and wet, and stuck to everything. By the time I got to Derby, the roads were getting slushy and sloppy, and harder to navigate. This whole case was beginning to remind me of a lake effect snowstorm. It was slushy, hard to navigate, and I had no idea how buried I would be before it was all through.

I pulled into the drive at Sharon Dellaplante's trailer, and slogged my way up to the door. I shook off the snowflakes that accumulated on my hair and shoulders on the short walk, and knocked on the door in the loudest way I knew. There was no immediate answer, so I rapped on the aluminum entry again. This time I could actually hear footfalls running to answer. I saw Maddy's face as she pulled back the drape covering the window in the door, and then heard the deadbolt unlock. She threw open the door and stared at me, stammering excitedly as she spoke.

"Banks! Oh, thank God, Banks! It's Sharon. She's been in bed since I got her home, and just a minute or two before you got here, I was making tea to bring in to her, you know calms the nerves and everything." Maddy was getting very animated by this time. "I went in to check on her, and she's not waking up!"

"Calm down, Maddy," I told her. "Did you call 9-1-1 yet?"

"Oh my God, no, I panicked, I didn't call anyone, I…"

"Maddy, call 9-1-1 right now, tell them you need an ambulance, give them the address. Do it now!" Maddy grabbed the phone and dialed. I went into the back bedroom, and saw Sharon on her side, covered by a white down comforter. Her knees appeared to be drawn up towards her chest, and she was making very shallow breathing sounds. Her eyelids were closed, and there was no movement under them, the way you might see if they were dreaming.

I took my gloves off and shoved them deep into my pockets, and reached to the side of her neck to feel for a pulse. It was there, slow

137

and weak, but there. I sighed audibly, and heard Maddy come in the room behind me. "She is still alive, isn't she?"

I looked at her, nodded, and she slumped against the doorway. I looked around the room, and noticed on the nightstand beside her bed there was a glass of water, about half full, and the white top of a prescription bottle. I looked around the area quickly to see if I could find the bottle, and I found it rolled halfway under the bed. It was a prescription for Elavil, a 30-day supply. The date on the bottle was today, and a quick count told me there were ten pills left. I looked up at Maddy, who was watching me from the door. She seemed to be assessing the situation, and then she put her hand to her mouth. She turned from the room, her shoulders hunched and shaking as she walked away. I could hear the siren of the ambulance outside, and I sat at the side of Sharon's bed until they brought everything into the room.

I gave the EMT's as much information as I knew, and they loaded her on to the gurney and took her out to the ambulance. When I asked where they were taking her, they said they were planning to take her to County Hospital, since they had a trauma unit and psychiatric floor. As soon as they left the room, I used a pencil to lift the pill bottle, put my gloves back on to lift the cover, and carefully slipped them into my coat pocket. I also managed to take the glass with the pencil, wrapped it in a handkerchief, and slipped it into my other coat pocket. Might be something, might be nothing, but I figured it might be worth checking them out.

I found Maddy hugging her knees in the trailer's living room. I put my hand on her shoulder. She looked up at me, here eyes puffy and red. "I had no idea," she said, shaking her head. "I had no idea she felt like this. Do you think she was trying to…" She buried her face in her knees, and began to rock.

"Did she talk about suicide or anything like that?" I asked her, wondering whether or not I was assuming the worst.

"No, she never said anything about wanting to kill herself," Maddy replied sniffling hard. I found some tissues in a box on an end table. I handed her a few, and she used them to wipe her eyes and nose.

LAKE EFFECT

"How was she handling things since the funeral?"

"Well," Maddy began, regaining her composure, "she said she felt responsible for the kid's deaths, that she should have taken better care of them, all that guilt shit most people go through."

"Had she been drinking at all? Had she taken anything else besides the Elavil?" I asked her.

Maddy shook her head no, and hung her head. At about that time, Kevin Garner showed up as the ambulance was leaving.

"What the hell?" he asked.

I met him in the kitchen and filled him in on what he missed. Sharon was on her way to County Hospital with an apparent prescription drug overdose, and Maddy was a basket case and not a lot of help. Kevin asked me if I called the senior Dellaplante, and I told him I hadn't notified the family at all yet. He said he would do it. I stepped outside on to the stairs off the kitchenette, and sucked in a lungful of cold wet air. I looked out at the snow, slowly accumulating in the driveway and on the road. I was beginning to contemplate a career in real estate, or used car sales.

Twenty-three

The lake effect snow machine managed to dump about 6 inches of the white stuff in the time I spent at Sharon Dellaplante's house. I swept the snow off the Jeep, and, just to be a nice guy, swept Garner's car while I was at it. I was beginning to regret ever having taken this case on. The good news is I think we could safely eliminate Sharon as the cause of death of her two babies. The bad news is that was as far as I could go with the good news. I still didn't know who, or why. I guess as far as Kevin was concerned, if I dropped the thing right now, he would be satisfied. The mother wasn't involved, and he paid her the money she was entitled to. But something was still very wrong in all of it. I knew it, and he knew it, too. He came out to his car as I was finishing it off.

"It has to be happy hour somewhere," he said, slapping me on the shoulder. I nodded, wincing at the pain the combination of cold and slap on my scarred shoulder caused.

"You buying, Mr. Insurance Investigator?" I asked.

"Sure," he said, forcing a smile.

We wound up at the Shoreline Inn, Kevin sipping a Grand Marnier neat. I was nursing a Killian's Irish Red Lager, thinking about Sharon. There was no conversation between Kevin and I for a long time, each wallowing in our own little pity parties. Finally, I broke the silence.

"So what happens next, Kev?" I asked him.

"As far as I know, from the company's point of view, the case is settled to the satisfaction of all parties," he said. "Will your report say anything to the contrary?"

I shook my head, and took a long drink from my glass.

"Then send me a final bill for time and expenses and we'll settle up with you, and probably keep you in mind for anything that comes up."

"Alright. Now, company line aside, what happens next, Kev?"

Kevin took a sip from his drink, and set it down on the bar between us.

"You are still working on the case, or you're a stubborn ass who hates loose ends. Which is it?" he asked.

"Both, but you know that. You said you sent out the check to Sharon. I saw a pile of mail on the kitchen table but nothing from Kellerman Insurance. Even given my basic mistrust of the mail services, it should have come with today's mail. A check that large should have come with a return receipt, right?"

"Yeah. So what are you getting at?"

"We both saw Sharon. Think she was out and about today, running errands and such?" I asked.

"Nope, not a chance."

"I agree. So, what are the odds she even answered the door and signed for the letter?"

Kevin nodded. "Keep going."

"So if it came today, and we assume that it did, someone else must have signed for it. And if someone else signed for it…"

"Someone else might have thought of cashing it," Kevin chimed in.

"Maybe," I said between sips of my beer. "But who and why?"

Kevin finished his drink, and waved the bartender for another. "I don't know."

"I can only think of two people for the who, maybe a third, but I still don't have a why."

"Ever think there may be no why?"

"What do you mean? People always do things for a reason. The reason may suck, or make no particular sense, but there is always a reason why. If you find out why, you eventually can get to who. But if I know who, that's not enough. I would still have to know the why." I drained the rest of my Killian's.

The Shoreline is one of those places that had been a half a dozen different places over the course of a couple of years. The interior has been about the same, dark paneling with dark furniture and a dark bar. Plus or minus a few pictures, trophies, and neon beer signs, the Shoreline Inn changed very little between owners. The snow falling outside kept all but the regulars out. Kevin and I had one

LAKE EFFECT

more, then split to go our separate ways.

Even with the snow-clogged streets and the panicked drivers, it didn't take very long to get to Carrie's house. I arrived at about the same time as a really pissed off Hamburg Pizza delivery guy. Heading him off at the pass, I paid him and rang the bell at the front door, carrying the boxes of food. Luckily for me, Paula answered the door. She flipped the porch light on, smiling at me, and opened the door.

"You call for a pizza, lady?" I asked, doing a bad New Yawker accent. I kicked the snow off my boots on the stoop before stepping inside.

"Uh-huh. Think you can deliver?" she asked seductively, wrapping her arms around my neck.

I put the pizza boxes on a small table in the foyer, and pulled her to me. "24/7, ma'am. Neither rain nor snow, nor..."

"Shut up," she said, kissing me deeply. She was right. I talk too much.

"Dadda!" Amanda shouted excitedly. She came flying around the corner and tackled my leg. The kiss deteriorated into mutual laughter. I bent down to pick up Amanda, and she immediately squeezed my neck hard and gave me a kiss on the cheek. "We didn't see you long time, Dadda."

"I know, honey, Daddy missed you and Kyle and Mommy very much. Where's your brother?" I asked her.

"Um, I think he here somewhere," she replied, looking around.

Suddenly a little voice from the background yelled, "Tupise, Dad! Tupise!"

"There's my little man," I said, kneeling down to catch him as he ran into me. I hugged both kids tightly, breathing them in like new life. The Hallmark moment was shattered when they got a whiff of dinner, sitting on the foyer table.

"Pizza!" they both shouted. Paula, amused at fleeting idolatry, laughed and guided them into Carrie's kitchen.

"All hail the conquering hero," Carrie called up from her basement. "Come to rescue me from these invaders, I hope." She

143

emerged at the basement doorway, carrying a load of freshly washed clothes in a basket.

"Hi, Carrie," I said, kissing her cheek. "Thanks for babysitting for me."

"Paula did all the hard work, I just cooked and cleaned and ..."

"And we appreciate it all," Paula chimed in. She cut up the pizza for Kyle and Amanda, while I got us a couple of pieces and diet sodas.

"What, no beer in the house?" I complained. It was a few minutes after that we were joined by Carrie's husband Jake and her two kids. They were older than Kyle and Amanda by a few years, but played with them all the same. They were as close as four cousins could be, and always made me glad that we had family near by for our kids to grow up with.

The four adults sat around the kitchen table, laughing and talking, feeling normal. It was good to feel normal again, and I realized how much I missed it. I missed my family, and it had only been a few days. Paula and I cleaned up the table, and turned Kyle and Amanda and their cousins loose on a small pile of toys in the living room.

"Hey, hon, do you think you could pull up the NPA website again for me?" I asked Paula, who was rinsing the pizza plates and putting them in the dishwasher.

"Sure, I think so. If Carrie will let us on the computer," she said. Carrie worked freelancing for a local marketing agency, and was very protective of her computer.

"As long as you keep Inspector Gadget here away from the keyboard," Carrie teased. "She doesn't respond well to the male touch."

"Are you inferring that your computer is a lesbian?" I asked.

"No, just that she prefers a gentle hand."

"He can do that," chimed in Paula, "but I don't want him wasting it on another woman."

"Defending my honor is very noble, and even a little sexy," I said, kissing Paula on the neck.

"Can't you two wait 'til you get home?" Carried asked,

LAKE EFFECT

exasperated at the public display of affection. We both smiled and agreed.

Paula, Carrie, and I moved to the makeshift office in a corner of her house. Kyle and Amanda played noisily in another room. Carrie powered her desktop computer up, and in a blur of keystrokes, Paula had the NPA Productions website on the screen. A few more clicks and she was able to pull up the list of overdue accounts, labeled as the "Deadbeat List". Apparently, NPA produces this list of clients to whom significant credit has been extended, and who have refused to pay the accounts within 30 days. This list is then sent to other online gaming companies, who may not allow the person on the list to wager at their site.

Paula looked intently at the list, and then spoke. "Something's missing," she said emphatically.

"What's missing?" I asked.

"A name. I saw it here the other day, and now it's gone. Hmmm, must have cleaned up the account, or something. Wait, there's another name missing. Now this is getting interesting. You'll never guess whose names are off the deadbeat list."

"Dellaplante and Lawrence," I sighed.

"Right you are. Say, are you a detective?" she teased.

"Not lately, but I am willing to learn."

We turned the computer off and debated the pros and cons of staying with Carrie or coming home. Carrie, of course, was willing to let the whole crew stay as long as they wished. I told Paula that I haven't found Victor Maloney, but that I didn't think he would be any direct threat to us anymore. In the end, I think it was her willingness to take a chance on me being right that lead to the decision to pack up the kids and go home. I felt better having them with me, and I think the kids were happy to be going to their own beds instead of the port-a-cribs they were consigned to at Carrie's.

"No more teepober at Aunt Carrie house?" Kyle asked.

"Nope," I laughed, scooping him up. "No more sleepovers."

On the way home, the kids sat quietly in their car seats, each playing with a toy from some kid's meal from someplace. Paula

145

asked me what I thought it meant that both Dellaplante and Lawrence were pulled from the deadbeat list at about the same time.

"I'm not sure, but it's a strange coincidence," I told her. "The check from Kellerman Insurance arrived today, allegedly, and then both guys have their debts wiped clean from an online gaming site."

"You don't believe in coincidence any more than I do," Paula said.

"Nope, not at all. There's a reason for everything."

"Then you need to have a reason to get the answer as to who actually killed them?"

"It'll help," I told her.

"Money's the oldest and most consistent motive I can think of," Paula stated.

"Jealousy, too."

"There's always jealousy, but whom, and of what?"

"Good question. Jealousy requires love. Somebody has it, somebody else loves it and wants it."

"Anybody in this whole scenario fit that description?" asked Paula as we pulled into the driveway.

I thought about that as we pulled our dozing children from their car seats and carried them as quietly as we could up stairs. Placing them in their own beds with a soft kiss goodnight, it was beginning to feel like normal once again. Paula and I crept carefully downstairs to our family room, holding hands as we tried to avoid making too much noise. I thought about what we talked about in the car. It occurred to me that what I needed to do was to see who fit into the most categories. I was still thinking about it as I sat down on the big overstuffed sofa, while Paula brought us in two glasses of wine. She sat down close to me, put her glass on the end table, and wrapped her arms around my neck. We looked at each other as if for the first time, and held each other tightly.

Twenty-four

Frank Dellaplante paced in his large den, his footfalls heavy on the hardwood floors. He stared out the window into the expanse of the night, the tree line barely visible under the quarter-moon's light as he thought back over the events of the day. Maddy had called him and he had spent the initial few hours at the hospital with Sharon, blustering and boasting to the doctors mostly, until he was ushered out by Maddy to the waiting area. When they had finally gotten her condition stabilized, he and his oldest daughter were allowed to see her in the intensive care ward. He could still smell the antiseptic in his nose, and see the flickering lines on the countless monitors telling him his little girl was still alive. When he stopped being a raging bull and started being a loving and concerned father, the nurses let him stay with her past the visiting hours. Maddy had left a few hours before he finally gave in to his own fatigue around 11pm.

Alone in the house, he found the quiet unusually disconcerting. Every sound reminded him of what he didn't have, and what he almost lost. Under normal circumstances, the quiet would have relaxed him, especially after a day on an earsplitting job site, with the pounding thunder of heavy equipment over the shrill screaming of power tools. Now it ridiculed him, the echoes making fun of all his possessions, all his worth. Because at the end of the day, he thought to himself, what did he have but his house, his company, and his children.

He walked over to the dry bar in the bookcase and poured himself a scotch in his used glass. He took a long drink of the dusky liquid, and winced as it heated the back of his throat. Dellaplante carried his drink back to the window to stare at the dark winter scenery, waiting for the sunrise. He would have to be at the office early in the morning to sign the papers on the sale of one of the excavators, and to make arrangements for the lease of another one to get it out to a site in Orchard Park. At least that takes care of some old debts, Dellaplante thought. He decided to look up the number for the local Gambler's Anonymous chapter, just because. Not that he would ever admit to a problem, but perhaps if he understood what other people went through, he could figure out what he could do for himself. Learn from their weakness, he figured.

Dellaplante paced the floor some more, thinking of his daughter Sharon. Why couldn't she be more like her sister Madeline? Maddy was strong, independent, levelheaded. Men respected her, and she took no shit from them. She reminds me of me, he thought. Sharon is too much like her mother was. Soft, sensitive, dependent on the love of other people to gauge her own worth, her mother was too good for this world. When she died of cancer, Dellaplante was left to raise two teenage daughters all on his own. He tried to teach his youngest to be more independent, to take nobody at face value, but she refused. She insisted on seeing the good in everyone, when clearly it was hardly ever the case. Then she got herself pregnant, not just once but twice, and still refused to listen. At least he was able to get her the job with the church, so she could have a little money coming in. She deserved better than that shitty little trailer she chose to live in, but the one foolish attribute she did learn was pride. She refused to live at home with Maddy, so she got what she could afford. Dellaplante smiled to himself. She is stubborn like her mother was, too.

He heard the garage door open, then the sound of a motor as a car pulled in slowly. The door between the kitchen and the garage opened brusquely, and Dellaplante heard the distinctive clicking of a pair of high heels on the ceramic tile floor. The sound grew gradually louder, changing timbre as the floor changed from tile to hardwood. He stood looking at the doorway to the den as Maddy started to walk past, then noticed him standing there. She was wearing a tailored black pantsuit with a red silk blouse, an outfit Frank was sure he had not seen before. But living in a house surrounded by women for all these years convinced him there was no way he could possibly know the inventory of any woman's closet, much less his fashion conscious daughter.

"Daddy? What are you still doing up?" she asked smiling. She walked over to him and placed an affectionate kiss on his stubbled

LAKE EFFECT

cheek.

"Hi honey, just a little trouble sleeping. I was thinking about your sister," he said. He thought he caught a scent of familiar cologne, but dismissed it.

"Any news?"

"None yet," he sighed. "But they haven't called with bad news, either."

"That's good, I guess," replied Maddy, shrugging her shoulders slightly.

"Where've you been tonight?" Frank asked, his arm around her shoulder as they walked into the hallway.

"Nowhere special, Daddy. I just met up with some friends at that new coffee shop in the village. I had all I could take of that hospital, with the tubes and the smell, and everything."

"I can certainly understand that, honey. It can get to you after a while. Awfully well dressed for coffee with the girls, aren't you?"

Maddy blushed. "You know how women can be. You have to look good even if you're going to a coffee klatch. You men really have it much easier, you know."

"I suppose. Your mother taught me long ago discussion of wardrobe is tantamount to a declaration of war."

"You are a wise man." She leaned up and in to kiss him again on the cheek.

"Flattery will of course get you everywhere," Frank said, smiling.

They ascended the stairs together, her arm linked in his. "Daddy, what do you think of that Banks guy you hired to find out who killed David and Sarah?" Maddy asked.

"He's like any of them, Maddy. He turns over rocks, and sees what happens. As far as I can tell, he's an arrogant, self-righteous, stubborn jerk, who might actually be good at what he does, and find out who is responsible for what happened to poor little Sarah and David."

"You really think so, don't you?"

"Yes I do. But right now, we have to be concerned with Sharon, and do whatever it takes to get her well. I blame myself for what she

149

did. I should have seen the signs, done more for her, and been there when she needed me." His eyes welled and his voice cracked.

Maddy rubbed his shoulder. "Daddy, don't beat yourself up over it. None of us saw it coming."

Dellaplante shook his head. "I could have seen it, if I was looking for it. Go to bed, honey," he said, kissing her forehead.

Twenty-five

I made a point of stopping by my favorite police department the next morning. Ramone was in his office, under a pile of paper as was his custom, when I dropped in with the medicine bottle and glass I lifted from Sharon's house.

"Jimmy, isn't it a little early to be this far behind in reports," I teased him.

"Yeah, you know," he sighed, "this place is every tree huggers worst nightmare."

"But just think of all the jobs you're helping to support in the lumber industry," I reminded him.

"Tell me you didn't stop out just to give me an early morning environmental update, Banks."

"Not at all. I need some forensics help here," I said, taking the glass, loosely wrapped in a white handkerchief, and placing it on the desk. "Got a plastic bag handy?"

Ramone handed me a plastic evidence bag. I turned it inside out over my hand and reached into my other pocket, grabbing the medicine bottle and cover. I pulled them out of my pocket, and handed the full bag back to Jim.

Ramone slipped a pair of rubber gloves out of his desk and put them on before taking the bottle out of the bag. "I assume prints?"

"Absolutely. I found them on the floor of Sharon Dellaplante's after she allegedly tried to commit suicide," I told him.

"You obviously don't think so," said Ramone, reaching behind his desk to grab an evidence bag. He slipped the bottle carefully into it and sealed it.

"The family believes it, but I have my doubts. You'll find partials of mine on there for certain, but I need to know who else handled the bottle."

"Done, I'll call you later, but we maintain control of the evidence, right?"

"Wouldn't have it any other way."

"By the way, did you find our boy Victor?" he asked.

151

"No, but I found out he has a friend in relatively high places," I informed him.

"What do you mean?"

"He and Michael Lawrence are old college chums," I said.

"Nobody, and I mean nobody, uses 'chum' anymore, boy," he corrected me.

"Fine, but you get the point. From what I was able to gather, they were together for a short time yesterday, and nobody's seen either one since about early to mid-morning."

"You puttin' two and two together?"

"Yup, and it's all starting to point to one guy."

"Well, I'll call you when the results are in."

I nodded, and then proceeded to head out to the Jeep. The morning air was crisp and cold, and unusually dry. I decided since I was having no luck catching up to Michael Lawrence, I would check in with his mother at the church rectory. Perhaps she could help me find him.

Around western New York, you get used to a very damp cold, like in New England, because of the Great Lakes. But this was nice, or at least as nice as January gets around Buffalo. The sun was bright, and the snow on the ground gave the day an extra shine. Winter can actually be beautiful, especially on days like this. The roads were drier than yesterday, and white with salt. It didn't take me very long to arrive at the rectory.

I rang the bell and Mrs. Lawrence appeared, looking every bit as stern and austere as the first time we met. She was again elegantly appointed, and again less than glad to see me. I have got to re-read Dale Carnegie some time.

"Mr. Banks, won't you come in out of the cold," she offered. I stepped into the vestibule, but the look she shot me did nothing to warm the air.

"Mrs. Lawrence," I acknowledged, nodding. "It's good to see you again."

"I highly doubt your sincerity in that statement, Mr. Banks. In fact, since you don't attend church, or at least not this one, I highly

LAKE EFFECT

doubt you would have any occasion to see me again unless you needed something from me. Please, let's dispense with the banter your type seems to enjoy so much. I have no time for idle chit-chat."

"That is disappointing, since you and I have become so close," I shot back. She responded with a look of indignation. "Then let's make it quick. Where can I find your son?"

"What do you want with Michael?" she asked me, showing a moment of concern.

"I need his help with a case I'm working on. Do you know where to find him?" I asked again, trying to put more urgency into the request.

"Does this have anything to do with the Dellaplante children, or with Sharon? I heard about her hospitalization yesterday. I think she's even being mentioned at Mass..."

"Mrs. Lawrence, for someone who was not anxious to talk to me you've become very chatty. Where's your son?" I asked, harshly. I felt guilty immediately after, but passed it off as a Catholic thing.

She looked at me as if she had a glass of cold water thrown in her face, eyes wide in disbelief. "He has his own place, Mr. Banks, over near Cloverbank," she said quietly.

I sighed. "Mrs. Lawrence, I believe your son is the link between the two children who were killed and a possible witness to the crime, who also died as a result of an extreme beating he took after talking to the police. I need to talk to Michael to find out what he knows and what he can tell me. If he knows something, and you prevent me from talking to him, I will have no trouble naming you as an accomplice to the police. They are aware of what I'm doing, and will be happy to do whatever is necessary in the name of justice to find the killers of those innocent babies." I was getting aggravated with having to justify myself to her, just to get a simple answer to a simple question.

"What do you want from me, Mr. Banks?" she asked, looking away.

"I want to find your son and talk to him. He's not in trouble at this point. I just have to talk to him." I was not going to leave

153

without an answer, and she knew it.

"He was at my house yesterday for a short time," she said, "then he left. He said something about going to do some ice fishing, but I didn't see him take any fishing poles or anything. He must have had them already in his truck. I don't know where he is, but I have some phone numbers, including his cell phone," she offered. I followed her back to her desk where she wrote out the numbers for me. I recognized one of them as the same one I found in Victor Maloney's pickup truck. I thanked her for her time, and left.

I called Sam at the office, hoping she'd be there. She was.

"Hey boss, how's Paula and the kids?" she asked cheerfully.

"Good. It's good to all be under one roof again. I need you to do me a favor, Sam. Give a call to that guy you know at the DMV, ask him to look up a registration for Michael Lawrence. He's officially getting hard to find, and he was last seen with Victor Maloney."

"Okay, but you will owe me," she said. "That guy's a little flaky, with a thing for tall redheads."

"That's what makes you perfect for this, kiddo," I told her. "Did you hear about Sharon Dellaplante overdosing last night?"

"It was in the paper this morning, just that she was rushed to the hospital, nothing about why," Sam answered.

"That was why. I happened to get there about the time Maddy said she found her."

"Are you thinking suicide or accidental OD?" she asked.

"I'm not sure at this point, but I managed to snag the prescription bottle before I left there, and dropped it off with Ramone at the Hamburg police station. So we'll see whose prints show up."

"Okay, I'll let you know what I come up with on this end. Where are you going now?"

"I thought I'd go check in on Sharon Dellaplante. It's getting close to visiting hours, so I want to check out what's going on, make sure she's okay, that sorta thing," I told her. It must be some sort of paternal instinct.

I hung up with Sam and went to the hospital. I stopped by the front desk, where they informed me Sharon had been moved to a

LAKE EFFECT

private room. Of course, I thought to myself, nothing's too good for the daughter of the infamous Frank Dellaplante. Taking the elevator to the correct floor, I found Frank and Maddy there as well. One of the nurses who recognized me from coming in to visit Casey waved to me from the station desk.

"Mister, Banks, right?" she asked. I nodded and smiled. "Does everyone you know wind up here?"

"Beginning to look like it, doesn't it," I replied sheepishly, and walked into Sharon's room. Both Dellaplantes turned to look at me, and Frank rose from his chair to head me off at the doorway.

"Maddy tells me you were there just after Sharon collapsed," he said matter-of factly.

"Right place at the right time, I guess," I said. "How is she doing?"

"The doctors are optimistic. They tell me the next 36 hours or so will be critical."

I looked past him and at the fragile girl in the hospital bed. A frightening array of tubes and bags, and wires obscured the view of an almost angelic, peaceful face. The sounds of artificial life support filled the room, audible in the background of everything that went on around her. Maddy had turned away, and had not looked back at me since I started talking to her father.

"How are you and Maddy doing?" I asked, turning my attention back to Frank.

He looked at me oddly. "What do you mean?"

"I mean are you two alright, is there anything I can do for you?"

"Why?" Maddy hissed. "All done investigating who killed David and Sarah? All set to take more money investigating who did this, too? I think you've done enough already, and that hasn't been shit so far!"

"Enough, Madeline!" said Frank, in a sharp but subdued voice. "We're doing fine, thank you for your concern. What have you found out about the children? Anything to believe the police can be called to make an arrest?"

"I have some witnesses that can place a man at the scene, and I am looking for that man now. The police had him in custody, but let

155

him go on bail before I could get the witnesses in to make an I.D."
Dellaplante looked like he needed good news, so I wanted him to
know something was going on. He nodded, acknowledging what I
was telling him.

"I know that the man I am looking for was at your office, and met
with Michael Lawrence. Do you possibly know where Lawrence
might be now?" I asked him.

"Maddy spoke with him most recently," he said, turning towards
his daughter. "Do you know where Mr. Banks might find him?"

"Do you think Michael has something to do with this?" asked
Maddy excitedly. There was more than a passing curiosity in her
voice. Her father shot her a quizzical look, than looked back at me
for my answer.

"I think I have some questions for him, since I haven't been able
to find the guy I, and the Hamburg Police, have been looking for," I
said.

"You call yourself a detective!" Maddy hissed. "The one guy
who couldn't possibly be involved in this mess and you think he's a
killer. Brilliant!"

"I never said he was involved," I corrected her patiently. "I said
he might know someone who is. All I do is ask questions. Oh, and
listen to the answers." I shot her a little wink and a smile, to which
she responded by sulking and turning her back. Lessons learned.

"I knew that smarmy son of a bitch must have had something to
do with this," Frank said. "He is supposed to be at the office, taking
care of an equipment sale I brokered to pay off some old debts. I'll
call him now." He started to pull a cell phone from his pocket, but I
reached out and stopped him.

"Don't. I'd prefer he didn't know I was coming."

Twenty-six

Maddy watched as her father and Banks went out of the room. She walked out of the room, past the two of them, and down the hallway to the common waiting area. There was a pay phone over to one side of the room, in a booth to protect the privacy of the loved one calling to update the family on a patient's condition. She walked across the room, entered the booth and started dialing.

"Dellaplante Development," the cheerful voice on the other end of the line chirped.

"Michael Lawrence, please," Maddy said softly, looking out the door of the booth.

"Excuse me?"

"Put Michael Lawrence on the phone or so help me I will rip your lungs out!" she spat into the phone.

"Oh, Miss Dellaplante, it's you. I'll get him."

It felt like forever, when she finally heard Michael's voice. "To what do I owe the honor?" he asked.

"Listen to me, Banks is coming over to see you. Now!" she said in hushed tones.

"No panic. He doesn't scare me in the least. He's nothing to us anymore," he said.

"He knows that that little prick Maloney was in to see you, and that you two know each other, and I don't know what else."

"Honey, relax. He's got nothing, and we have nothing to worry about," Lawrence said, trying to calm her.

"Michael, there's something else. I went to clean up after the ambulance, and I couldn't find the medicine bottle. Did you take it?"

"Medicine bottle?" Lawrence asked, concerned.

"Yeah," she said mockingly. "Small, brown, you put pills in it, take pills out."

"Smart ass, I know what a medicine bottle is. What do you mean you can't find it? I put it on the nightstand before I left."

"You may have thought you did, but you didn't, and now I can't

157

find it," she responded frantically.

"Okay, calm down a minute. When did you see it last?" he asked her.

Maddy thought about it for a second or two. "I went in to check on Sharon just before Banks showed up…"

"Banks!" Lawrence interrupted. "Goddamn it! I'll bet anything the sonovabitch took it with him when he left."

"Why the hell didn't you get rid of that thing when you had the chance?" she asked venomously.

"Me? Why not you, or are you too used to having people do your shit work for you?" he responded.

"I don't need this, Michael!" She was starting to get loud, and some people who had found their way into the waiting area were starting to stare. She felt their eyes on her, and turned her back to the door. "Listen to me, if Banks already has you connected to that little shithead Maloney, and has the medicine bottle we emptied into my dear sister, then we are screwed. Do I make myself clear to you?"

"Crystal clear, darling. What do you suggest?"

"I don't want to have to worry about this at all any more, Michael," she purred. "Do what you think is best."

"Haven't I taken care of everything for you so far?" Lawrence asked.

"Mmmm, and haven't I always shown the proper appreciation?" she asked, smiling shamelessly.

"Yes you have, babe, and don't worry you pretty little head about it. I'll take care of that pain in the ass, Banks. He won't be bothering us anymore."

"Will I see you tonight, lover?" Maddy asked.

"Absolutely."

She hung up the phone, smiling to herself, and pushed the booth door open. She looked up to see Banks and her father walk past the doorway to the waiting area. She waited a moment or two, and watched for her father to walk back towards Sharon's room. As he did she caught up to him, her hands thrust in her pockets, and she

LAKE EFFECT

quickly matched his stride.

"Why do you insist on paying for his services? It's such a waste of money," she said.

"He is good at what he does, and he is a man who believes in causes. That's what keeps him going, not the money," Dellaplante explained. "At this point, I could stop paying him and he still wouldn't give up. He is what I used to refer to as a bulldog."

"Why does Banks think Michael Lawrence is involved? I mean, he and Sharon were close. You don't think he would hurt her children, do you?" she asked.

"Honey, you don't know Lawrence the way I do," he told her, his voice full of hate. "I wouldn't put it past him at all. He probably wants to make a big score and take off with the money, and I wouldn't be at all surprised to find he had a hand in driving poor Sharon to suicide."

"You're probably right, Daddy," she said.

Twenty-seven

I knocked on the door to Michael Lawrence's office, and pushed it open when I didn't hear a response from the other side. I saw him sitting behind his desk, writing something on a yellow notepad. When he looked up and spotted me, he shoved everything to one side, turning the pad over.

"You really should answer your voice mail messages once in a while, Michael," I said to him, moving towards a chair on one side of his desk. "I've been trying to call you for a couple of days now."

"Yeah, well, I've been busy lately. Still am, so what do you want?" he asked.

"So tell me about Victor Maloney," I said as I sat across the desk from him. His office was about as austere as Frank Dellaplante's, with the exception of some Buffalo Bills memorabilia here and there. He was dressed for work in an office, not a construction site, and looked oddly out of place in his tailored suit. He should have been working downtown in an executive office somewhere, not here where the smell of diesel hung in the frigid air, and the signs of mud tracking permeate the all-weather carpeting.

"Is that the creep who was following me? It figures," Lawrence said, leaning back in his chair and looking out towards the narrow window into the equipment yard.

"You know him, you had coffee with him the other day, according to Cyndi," I told him, waiting for a response.

He shot me a quick glance and thought for a minute before looking back out the window into the yard. " Okay, yeah, he came by to see me. We know each other from high school. He was looking for work, trying to help pay for college, you know. He thought I could help him get a job for the summer between semesters." Lawrence was still looking out the window, not paying me any attention.

"So you were just helping an old school buddy out? Were there a lot of graduating stalkers in prep school, Mike?" I asked him.

He turned his attention sharply back towards me. "What are you trying to say?"

161

RONALD W. ADAMS

"Michael, I've got this job, see, as a private investigator. It's my job to find things out for people, even if it's only for me sometimes, and even if it's stuff that I don't really want to know. So I look into our friend Victor, and I find out he is the son of John Francis Maloney, attorney at law. And I find out that his bill is paid for at the school, thanks to Daddy. So the money for school thing doesn't work for me. So what did Victor stop by to see you about? Really?"

"Like I said," Lawrence said, his face reddening slightly. He was getting pissed off, which was good for me.

"Just asking," I said, smiling. "By the way, how did his face look?"

"Like somebody hit him with a baseball bat."

"Or a flashlight, whatever. Now why don't you tell me about Victor, so I can move on to bigger and better things."

"Look, Banks, I help people out when I can. Victor was a freshman when I was a senior, and I helped him get a try-out for the varsity hockey team. In college, I helped him pledge the same fraternity I was in," Lawrence explained. "I don't know what I did to piss him off, or anything else. I've always been nice to the guy, and for some reason he wants to make my life miserable. I'm sure in your line of work you deal with all types of assholes."

I looked directly into his eyes. "All the time," I told him, smiling. "But it troubles me that you were the last person to see Victor."

"How do you know that?" he shot back.

"Mike, the word after 'Private' on my card says 'Investigator'. Trust me on this one."

He didn't handle the sudden onset of sarcasm well. I don't blame him, but I was trying to push him. A good liar can be entertaining, even amusing under the right circumstances. He was lying badly, and I hate a bad liar.

"Alright, Sherlock. He met me here, we went out for coffee, I took the day off to be with Sharon, and he just took off. End of story," he told me, sharply.

"Did you stop by the pharmacy to pick up her prescription?" I asked.

LAKE EFFECT

"Yes, I mean, well, she, or I mean her sister asked me to pick it up since I was coming over." If he had stammered any harder he would have resembled a well-dressed Porky Pig. He looked away from me and looked out the window again. "If I had known what she was going to do with it, I never would have…"

"She whom, Sharon or Maddy?" I interrupted.

"Sharon, of course," he said, turning quickly from his poignant window gazing. "What are you saying, that Maddy forced her to take the whole bottle at once?"

"Nope, didn't say that at all. But since you brought it up, how did you know it was the whole bottle? And what makes you think Maddy gave it to her?"

He glared at me again. The funniest thing I have noticed about fair-haired people is that their ears tend to get red when they're angry. And Lawrence was no exception. "What exactly are you saying, Banks?" he asked, straining to achieve a level of composure.

"Just asking questions. It's what I do," I answered, matter of factly.

"No, I think what you do is take money for doing nothing. You took money from the insurance company, and you didn't find the killers. You are taking money from old man Dellaplante, who needs all the money he's got to take care of his business, and you still don't got shit, Banks!"

"Michael, please, your language," I said, feigning sensitivity.

"Get out right now you smug son of a bitch, or so help me I will kick your ass."

"Michael, Michael. You would try, you would get hurt really badly, and you would only get yourself more upset than you already are," I explained to him as gently as possible. "Tell Victor I'm looking for him."

"What makes you think I'll be seeing him again?" he asked.

"I don't, but if you do, pass the message on."

"Are you through?"

"I think so. I got the answers I was looking for," I said turning towards the door. "Oh, one more thing. How long have you and

163

Maddy been sleeping together?"

"What?" he said, loudly.

"I was just wondering if you made a clean break from Sharon before you started screwing her sister." Most people would have been content to just say good-bye, but I couldn't resist testing him one more time. Besides, I had to see if my assumption was correct. From the look on his face, I may as well have slapped him with a horseshoe. It was an expression of shock, disbelief, and anger. Lots and lots of anger.

"Get the fuck out of here!" he shouted.

"I'm going. Thanks for a lovely chat, Michael. I'll be in touch." I closed the door behind me.

I walked out into the lobby area to grab my coat. Cyndi, my favorite receptionist was there, smiling and perky as ever. She looked at me with eyes wide and said, "Gee, Joe. He sounded really mad at you. What were you two talking about?"

I leaned on her desk as I put my coat on. "We were discussing who was a better coach for the Sabres, Lindy Ruff or Ted Nolan," I explained, smiling back at her.

"I didn't know Mikey, uh, Mr. Lawrence, was a hockey fan. I thought Ted Nolan was cute," she said.

"You know what, that's exactly what Mikey said," I told her.

Behind me, down the hallway, I heard a door slam shut.

"Wow, he must really be a Ted Nolan fan," sighed Cyndi. I smiled and nodded.

Twenty-eight

I was on my way down Route 20 heading back towards Hamburg when the cell phone rang. As I held the steering wheel with one hand and a knee, I vowed to get one of those hands-free set-ups one of these days.

"Banks," I answered.

"You know, I can't get used to you answering the phone like that," Paula said, chuckling. "It sounds too tough for you."

"Hey, you know me, winning through intimidation. What's up, hon?"

"We have a problem at the house. The sun is melting the snow and ice is jamming up the gutters," she explained.

"Is it pulling the gutter away from the house?" I asked nervously. That happened at another house we lived in, and it wasn't something I wanted to repeat.

"No, not yet. I wanted to let you know I'm going to call the contractor we used for the deck last year to come and check it out."

"That'd be good. Hopefully they can come out sooner rather than later."

"I'll let you know. You gonna be late tonight, hon?" she asked.

"Shouldn't be."

"See ya for supper."

"What are you making?" I asked her.

"Since when does the menu matter?" she asked playfully. "Besides, you're gonna wanna be here for dessert."

"I am?"

"Uh-huh," she whispered breathily. "See ya soon."

"Now how am I supposed to work after that?" I asked her, with a combination of anticipation and frustration.

"Your problem, Banks. Just get home when you're done." I love it when she's bossy. Come to think of it, I love it even when she's not bossy.

I hadn't been to the office yet today, so I grabbed a couple of cups of coffee at the doughnut shop before going there. Sam was

165

hard at work, doing the latest crossword puzzle in the newspaper. I suppose it would be cheaper to buy an answering machine, but then who would I get to go for bagels once in a while? She looked up long enough to see that I brought coffee, popped the plastic top off the paper cup, and took a sip. She smiled, and then went back to her puzzle.

"Remind me again why I pay you instead of getting a machine to take messages?" I asked, moving to my desk.

"Because I'm cuter, more clever, and will go for bagels once in a while," she said. She had me there.

"Any messages?" I asked.

"Uh-huh. One from Kevin Garner, just to call him back when you get a chance," she read from a small stack of message slips. "Another one from Kevin, one from the telephone company, the cell phone company, one from Paula. Did she call you?"

"Yup, just a few minutes ago. Anything else?"

"Let's see. Here's one from the landlord, wanting to know about the rent check, if it was legitimate. I told him I asked you the same thing about my paycheck, and assured him it was," she grinned.

"Thanks for the back-up," I told her.

"That's what I'm here for. Oh, and a Mr. John Francis Maloney called for you. He didn't leave a message, said you would know what it's about. What's it about?" she asked.

"Father of the kid who broke into my house. He can't find him, and neither can I."

"He sounded, well, kinda upset if the truth be told."

"I'll try him first, maybe he's heard from him."

I looked up the number to the house, and from the housekeeper got the phone number to his office. I called the office and heard the receptionist say quickly, "Maloney and Maguire, please hold."

Instant silence, followed by the news courtesy of the local public radio station flooded my right ear. At least it wasn't Muzak, to which I believed myself to be terminally allergic. After what must have been a minute or so, the receptionist came back on the line. "Maloney and Maguire, how may I direct your call?"

LAKE EFFECT

"Mr. Maloney, please," I said as pleasantly as possible.

"I'm sorry sir, but Mr. Maloney is taking no calls today. Please try back tomorrow."

"I'm returning his call from earlier this morning," I explained, trying to put some authority behind the words. "My name is Banks, and if you tell him I'm holding, I'm sure he'll take the call."

"Please hold," she said, giving me another opportunity to listen to public radio news. I suppose I couldn't expect Stevie Ray Vaughn in an attorney's office.

"Mr. Banks, I'm glad you called," said Maloney.

"I just got your message. Have you heard from your son?" I asked.

"No, I haven't. I was hoping you had some information you could share with me. I'm starting to get nervous."

"I understand. I spoke to someone about him earlier today, but the person told me they parted company early and he hasn't seen him since."

"He has a court date, and we posted the bail money to ensure he would appear," Maloney said, with a growing sense of urgency in his voice. "Do you know how it would look if my son failed to show for a court date?"

"Excuse me," I said, shaking my head in disbelief. "What do you mean how it would look?"

"Mr. Banks, try to understand, we have a very large, very prominent role in the legal community," he tried to explain. "It was bad enough that my son was arrested for breaking and entering. Specifically into your home, as I understand it. But now this inexcusable, blatant disregard for legal authority, running away like some common..."

"Excuse me," I said into the phone, interrupting. "I hate to interrupt your sermon, and really, it was a very good one, but aren't you forgetting a little something, counselor?"

"What?" he asked, annoyed that someone knocked him off his verbal stride.

"Has it occurred to you that perhaps someone might be preventing him from being found?"

"What are you saying, Banks?"

"Mr. Maloney, I know you're this wonderful attorney, fighter for the oppressed and all that. But your son's world was and is very different from yours. He was working for someone who thought nothing of paying him to break into my house and hurt me and my family, and he was willing to do it. There is a distinct possibility that these same people would have no problem hurting him if they thought he turned from an asset to a liability." The silence on the other end of the phone was thick and palpable. He understood exactly.

"Mr. Maloney, I have two kids of my own, and the reason I even know anything about your son is because I am investigating the deaths of two other children," I went on. "No parent wants to think their kid is the school bully, or the bad guy."

"I don't know what to say, Mr. Banks," he said, barely above a whisper. "I suppose I'll let you know when I hear from him."

"Likewise," I said, just before hearing the click of disconnection on the line."That went well," said Sam sarcastically behind her newspaper.

"Who asked you," I said wearily.

"Tell me you are not gonna help that guy find his missing delinquent son."

"Nah. Let him straighten out his own house. Besides, how would it look if I took a missing persons case on a kid who broke into my house?"

"Conflict of interest?" she asked, knowing the answer

"Oh yeah.""So how's the Dellaplante girl doing?"

"She's not out of the woods yet, but everyone seems optimistic," I said, not real convincingly.

"But?" Sam asked."I'm not sold on the suicide theory."

"It doesn't fit with the whole 'she killed her kids for the money' scenario, which you didn't believe either," Sam observed.

"No, it doesn't."

"Which means you think someone tried to kill her, too," she said."Say, you are getting good at this, aren't you?"

"Great minds, you know. After all, I am your investigative

168

LAKE EFFECT

assistant," she said with a cheesy grin.

I had to laugh. She had been hanging around me far too long.

"So, if you think someone tried to take out Sharon Dellaplante, what's the next step? Any suspects?" Sam asked, finally putting the newspaper aside.

"Two, but I'm not sure how I can prove it. It's gonna depend on whose fingerprints show up on a prescription bottle and a water glass, and whether or not Sharon recovers," I explained.

"Which one are we counting on first?"

"I'm praying for both," I told her.

Twenty-nine

I did finally make it home in time for supper, which was well worth it. Not that the meal was anything to brag about to a gourmet chef, but no gourmet could ever match Paula's lasagna. Nor could any five star restaurant anywhere in the country match the ambience of dinner with two year olds at the kitchen table. The combination of happy kids and spaghetti sauce made me glad it was bath night, and glad the whole family was back together. Who would have thought I'd be nostalgic about this kind of chaos.

Paula and I did the dishes while Kyle and Amanda went back to serious playtime with building blocks and toys trucks. I could tell she wanted to ask me about the progress on the Dellaplante case, but wasn't sure she should. I broke the ice by telling her about my visit to the hospital to see Sharon Dellaplante. I opted not to tell her about my suspicions about who put her there. Instead I figured I would concentrate on the topic of home repair.

"So, did you get a hold of the contractor about the gutter," I asked her.

"Umm, yeah, I did. Said he'd be out in a day or so. Not too much he could do 'til all the ice is off the roof," she explained, drying the lasagna pan and putting it in the cabinet under the counter.

"Oh, okay. If this thaw keeps going, maybe he'll be here before too long," I said, feeling more awkward in avoiding the hot topic than confronting it.

"Yeah, that's, uh… oh for God's sake, Joe, what the hell are we doing?" Paula asked, exasperated by the polite evasion. She stood facing me, leaning against the counter with her hands on her hips, demanding more than I had given her.

"You're right. I'll tell you all that's going on after we put the kids down tonight, okay? I promise," I told her, and leaned in to give her a kiss.

"You better. This thing has gotten much bigger, and I'm involved since someone broke into my house. Whether you think I should

171

know or not, I have a right to know."

"Yes, you do. Besides, maybe looking at this thing with new eyes will help me figure it out. Let's finish up here, and go play with Kyle and Amanda for a while. Then we'll talk." Paula nodded in agreement.

We finished the dishes and went into the family room to play with the kids for a while before bath time. More play time in the tub, this time with Mom and Dad providing perfect targets for splashing. Once they were cleaned up and dried off, there was time for a book, usually one of their favorite Mercer Mayer books, then bedtime. Paula and I usually fall into a state of collapse about then, but this time we were both too anxious. She needed to hear what was going on, and in truth, I really needed to tell her.

"Here's what I have," I started. "Sharon Dellaplante is in the hospital from an apparent overdose of Elavil. Victor Maloney, the charming guy who broke into our house, and the prime suspect in not one but three murders, David and Sarah Dellaplante, and Casey Kasparczak, is missing. Victor is also an old school buddy of Michael Lawrence."

"Okay," Paula said, absorbing the information as I went along. "Do you think Michael Lawrence is involved in the Dellaplante case, too?"

"I didn't at first, but now I'm beginning to think he is. And I'm beginning to wonder about Sharon's sister, Maddy."

"Why's that?"

"Too many things that seem odd," I explained, as much for myself as for Paula. "For example, Lawrence's name was taken off the deadbeat list about the same time as the insurance payment was made to Sharon. And when I mentioned Michael to Maddy today, she got very defensive."

"Joe," Paula reminded me, "Frank Dellaplante's name came off about the same time."

"True, but he sold equipment to raise the cash. What did Lawrence sell to raise money?"

"Okay, you got that one. Now what about Maddy and Lawrence?"

172

LAKE EFFECT

Paula asked. Her wheels were in full motion, eager to pitch in to help.

"I mentioned wanting to talk to Lawrence, and Maddy exploded on me like he would be the last person on earth that would be capable of a crime."

"She's protecting him, or she thinks she is," Paula said.

"I thought so, too. That's why I asked Lawrence how long he'd been sleeping with her," I said.

"Real subtle," Paula said, stifling a laugh. "That must have gone over real well."

"Crude but effective. You should have seen the look on his face."

"I bet. So, we think Maddy Dellaplante and Michael Lawrence are having an affair," Paula repeated.

"Correct."

"And Lawrence is friendly with this Victor Maloney, so there is some guilt by association there."

"Correct," I said one more time.

"And based on this information we can assume what?" she asked.

"I'm hoping to find out the results of a fingerprint match. If Sharon's prints aren't on a medicine bottle filled by her pharmacy the day of the overdose, then she had more help with her medicine than is legally required," I explained.

"But how does this tie into the murder of the Dellaplante children, and your buddy Casey?" Paula asked.

"Well, my two lakeside informants can place Victor Maloney at the scene of the murder at Locksley Park, and another can place him as Casey's attacker, and hopefully he could tell us who his accomplice was."

"That's good. But what about Maddy and Lawrence?"

"The way it looks to me, they were trying to get rid of Sharon," I told her.

"You think the father of her babies and her own sister were going to poison her?" she asked, her mouth still open in surprise.

"They had two hundred thousand reasons to do it."

"Tempting reasons," she said. "Is money really thicker than

173

blood?"

"With these two, I'm not sure they make the distinction."

Thirty

At Sharon Dellaplante's trailer, Maddy rolled over under the covers and placed her hand gently on Michael's bare chest. He moaned softly as she slowly stroked her fingers lightly over him. Lawrence began to stir at her touch, rolling over to face her, and opened his eyes.

"Are we not planning on sleeping at all tonight?" he asked her, draping his arm over her hip.

"Are we too tired to go again?" she asked, playfully kissing his chin.

"You are too much," he said, rolling her on to her back, kissing her fully on the lips.

"I'll give her this much, Sharon has a very comfortable mattress," Maddy giggled, bouncing her hips up and down. "Lots of rebound."

"And we both know what that's good for, don't we," said Lawrence pinning her beneath him. They kissed feverishly, reveling in the sinful pleasure of their rendezvous.

After a few moments, Maddy broke the kiss. "Listen, Michael, what are we going to do about Banks?"

"What do you mean?" he asked.

"He's getting too close. He's a smart guy, and he's gonna ruin everything."

Lawrence rose up on his elbow, looking down at his lover. "I think you're overreacting, Maddy. He's got nothing concrete, and he can't go to the police with suspicion and innuendo."

"Maybe, Michael. But what if he did grab that medicine bottle? We never found it, and I'm scared he did."

"So what?" he said. "I mean, if he found it, and if our fingerprints are on it, there's no big deal. All it proves is we touched the bottle, it doesn't mean we did anything illegal with it."

"That's still taking a big chance," she said, snuggling in closer to him. She knew he would do what she wanted, if she just kept at it. All men were like that, all so eager to please for the right reward.

She caressed his naked body with her own. "Besides, I was right about Maloney, wasn't I?"

"Yes, you were. We are definitely better off without him."

"He was an idiot, anyway. You would never wind up getting caught like that. I can't believe you trusted him to scare off Banks by breaking into his house," she said, sounding disappointed in his decision. "He thought he was so big and tough, with his precious Mommy and Daddy to bail his ass out if he got caught. He would have told them everything, gladly even, to save himself." She was getting to him, she could tell by the way his body was responding to hers.

"But he's not a consideration now, is he?" Lawrence asked her rhetorically between soft kisses. "No need to worry about him any more."

"No, but we now have to consider Mr. Banks." She continued smiling 'at him seductively.

"Don't worry," said Michael in a semi-whisper. "I'll have a talk with him in the morning sometime. I'm sure I can persuade him he's going the wrong way with his little investigation."

"And if you can't?" Maddy asked, smiling, daring him to answer her. She was truly enjoying the power she had over Lawrence. He was almost as easy to play as her father, and much sexier and satisfying.

"Well then, we'll just have to see what happens", he said, kissing her ardently, ending further discussion.

Thirty-one

At the office the next morning, I settled in to return some phone calls. There were some people who were waiting patiently, and a lot who weren't, to get paid their past due bills. After doing my best to placate the maddening throng, I sank into the chair to tend to the mundane task of following up and writing the checks I promised. A task made much easier by the fact that I had paying customers, for a change. Sam wandered in, bearing coffee and doughnuts, bringing in the chill of the early morning with her. Coat off, food and drink properly distributed with the requisite thanks, and like clockwork the phone rings. "Banks Investigations," she answered. "Yes, he is as luck would have it. Can you hold for a minute please?" She pushed the hold button, and turned to me and said, "There's a John Francis Maloney on the phone, says you and he spoke about his son. Victor?"

"Yup, that's dear old dad. I'll take it," I told her as I took the phone from her hand. "Mr. Maloney, what can I do for you?"

"Mr. Banks, thanks for taking my call," said Maloney. "I have been doing a lot of thinking lately, especially about how well I know my son."

"Have you heard from him, sir?" I asked respectfully.

"No, I haven't, not yet anyway. Do you know whether or not my son killed the man the police say he did?" he asked fearfully.

"I have witnesses that say he did."

"And you believe he is involved somehow with Michael Lawrence."

"Yes, I think he and Lawrence are connected to another case I'm working on."

"And he broke into your house. Was anyone hurt?"

"Just your son," I told him.

"Yes, and I thank you for not killing him. I don't know you, or anything about you, but I know you would have legally been within your rights to shoot him if you had a gun," he said, hiding behind convenient legal-speak.

RONALD W. ADAMS

"True, and I do own a gun, but really, who needs the mess and the paperwork hassles?" I joked, trying to lighten things up a little. It didn't work.

"Mr. Banks, I'm not calling as a lawyer but as a father who's concerned about his son," Maloney said. "As a lawyer, I would do everything under the law to protect the rights and privacy of my client. As a father, I want to help you find my son, and make sure he's safe."

"I can appreciate that, but you have to understand that I'm looking for him only in as much as he's involved in another investigation."

"Yes, the Dellaplante murders, I've read about them in the papers. I thought the insurance company investigation cleared the mother of any wrongdoing?"

"Finding out who didn't do it isn't the same as finding out who did," I explained.

"I understand that, and I'm glad to hear you say it. I believe I am getting a good picture of the type of person you are," he said.

"Should I be pleased or worried by this?" I asked him, again trying to lighten things up. He was trying to make a point, and I wanted him to relax and get to it.

"Pleased, I hope. Anyway, as a lawyer, anything I found that might be considered evidence would be held pending a warrant. As a father, however, I have something that may help you find Victor's whereabouts."

"I'm listening," I told him.

"Victor keeps appointments in a black day planner, a gift from his mother when he started college so he could keep a study schedule. Both he and his mother are compulsive about keeping a schedule, and writing everything down in their planners. I will send it via courier to you this morning," he said.

"Why not send it to the police? I'll wind up sharing it with them eventually, anyway," I told him.

"I'm sure you will, but I believe you will try to find Victor first, then do what you have to after." He sounded resigned to the fate of his son, as if he didn't expect this to end well. I shared his emotion,

178

LAKE EFFECT

and felt empathetic.

We finished our discussion, and I sincerely felt for the guy. I know Paula and I are trying to do the best we can with Kyle and Amanda, but even at that, would it be enough. I don't know how this Victor was brought up, or what factors influenced his truly poor choices. But I found myself hoping that when the time comes, our kids would be at least equipped to make the right decisions in their lives. Every parent's hope and dream, and every parent's nightmare rolled into one.

It was a surprisingly short time before the courier showed up with the planner. I took it back to my desk, and read slowly everything Victor had written down. From what I could tell, the kid had a serious issue with documentation. Paula was the most organized person I knew, with Sam coming in a close second, but even they didn't keep this tight a schedule, or have records this meticulous of their everyday activities. Not only were there class appointments and assignments, and doctor's appointments, but dates with girlfriends, trips to the laundromat, library, and fast food joints. There were notes about each of the trips to everywhere and nowhere. The thought that there may be enough noteworthy things happening in this kid's life was surprising enough without adding the further thought that in his own mind he believed it all worthy of keeping record. What is an attorney, or an attorney to be, without a healthy ego?

This planner was set up to follow the school year, September to August. That was a break, because I was able to start in December and work backwards and forwards to figure out how our boy came in contact with whomever. Starting in September, just after Labor Day, until just after Christmas, I noted the entry "Meet with M.L." no less than 45 times. And after New Years Day, there was only one entry of any type in the journal and that was just two days after Mr. Maloney was arrested for breaking into my house. The entry was "Meet with M.L."

I got up, crossed the office, and poured a cup of coffee from a pot Sam made an hour ago. Unlike fine cheese, fine wine, and myself, fine coffee does not age well. As I stirred the cream and sugar into it, I thought more about the eerie ending to Victor Maloney's planner. Someone who took pains to document every aspect of their life the way this guy did wouldn't just stop for no apparent reason. There was not going to be a happy ending for Victor's father, and I had a feeling it was going to end badly for Michael Lawrence as well.

I returned to find Sam in my chair, perusing the planner. I grunted and nudged, trying to pry her from her current perch, and she did what any woman or cat would do in her position. She ignored me. "Look at this," Sam said, pulling a pencil from behind her ear. "He has an entry here on the day the Dellaplante kids were kidnapped."

'Meet ML', it said in red ink. The time slot he started it on was 8:00pm, and the return time was ten o'clock that night.

Thirty-two

Sam continued reading while I got Jimmy Ramone on the phone. There was a need to share this with him, and to find out what he had on the fingerprints. I hoped he was in a sharing mood.

"Ramone," he said sharply as he answered his phone.

"Hey, it's Joe Banks, how ya doin' Jimmy?" I said as cheerfully as I could. I read once that people are more inclined to give you what you need if you are pleasant in asking.

"No time, Banks," he said abruptly. So much for that theory, I thought.

"Having a bad day, are we? Just tell me what you found on the medicine bottle and glass, Jim. Did your guys at least process them?"

Annoyed, he shot back, "What kind of jerk-offs do you think we have working here? Yeah, we processed it. All kinds of prints on the bottle, including yours. On the glass, just one set."

"I'll bet you a beer at Fitzgerald's Pub that they weren't Sharon Dellaplante's, were they?"

"No they weren't," he said. "Since the county went to fingerprint I.D. for their clients on assistance, we checked there. We matched the prints on the glass against all known fingerprints in Erie County Department of Social Services files and came up with nothing. Now, what do you have for me?"

"Victor Maloney's day planner slash journal. Including meetings with a 'ML' detailed out, it makes for an interesting read," I told him. "It could be coincidence, but I believe it stands for Michael Lawrence. It's worth checking out, especially since I've established they know each other, and since I know they met on at least one other occasion mentioned in the planner."

"You got it how, this day planner?" he asked. It amazed me how much conversation takes place after you get told they don't have time to talk.

"Victor's father, trying to do the right thing, in hopes we'll find his son," I explained to him.

"Uh-huh. Gonna bring it by or do you want me to come out and pick it up?"

"That all depends. Do you have time to come to the office, or are you still too busy to talk to me?"

"Dammit, Banks. Quit screwin' around, will you!" he yelled into the phone.

"You quit screwing around, Jimmy. Telling me you got no time to talk makes you sound like an arrogant prick, and I know you're neither. We help each other, we don't piss on each other."

"Alright, Mr. Sensitive, I got you. I'll be out to your office after my shift."

"Great, see you then," I said, hanging up.

That gave me a few hours to figure out what to do next. The only other person that could have come in contact with the glass was Maddy Dellaplante. It would make sense that those would be her prints, but what does that prove? The only thing I could think to do would be to see if I could get either Maddy or Michael Lawrence to tell me what is going on. It seemed to me they were the only two that made any sense at all being involved in this whole mess. I hadn't quite given up on Victor Maloney, but I was losing hope of getting to talk to him in person.

Sam finally broke the silence, told me she was heading out to grab some lunch, and did I want anything. I wasn't feeling really hungry, so I just asked her to stop for coffee on the way back. I was still too absorbed in my thoughts to hear the door shut behind her as she left. I picked up the phone and called Dellaplante's house, and asked for Maddy.

"I'm sorry, Mr. Banks," said the housekeeper, "but Miss Dellaplante is at the hospital with her sister at the moment. May I take a message?"

"No, thanks, no message. But maybe you could tell me how long ago she left?" I asked her.

"Well, I think it was about a half hour ago, around there. I know she said she had an errand or two to run and that she would be at the hospital for the rest of the afternoon."

LAKE EFFECT

"Thank you very much, ma'am", I said, hanging up. At least I could catch her there. Maybe it wasn't the best place to confront someone, but I'll take the chance when I can. There were too many unanswered questions for me, and I sort of felt like I owed something to Sharon. While I waited for my coffee, I figured I would call Lawrence and ask him about Victor, see what he had to say. It would be just a friendly conversation between two guys to see if one of us was a murderer.

"Dellaplante Development," answered Cyndi.

"Hi Cyndi, it's Joe Banks. How are you?" I asked cheerfully.

"Oh, hi!" she said in recognition of my name. "How are you?"

"Great, kiddo. Say, is Mike Lawrence in?"

"Yeah, he is. Are you two gonna be talking about hockey again?"

I laughed involuntarily. "You know guys, Cyndi, all we talk about are sports and chicks."

"Really?" she asked, surprised that I would share this rare insight into the male psyche. The more I spoke to Cyndi, the more I began to appreciate Sam.

"No, not really. May I talk to Mike, please?"

"Oh, Joe. Yes, hang on."

Lawrence came on the line. "What can I do for you?" he asked.

"Just a couple of questions, if you have the time," I told him.

"Alright, but I'm very busy. We have a zoning board meeting in Amherst in 15 minutes."

"It won't take a second. You told me, if I'm not mistaken, that Victor is an old school friend who was hitting you up for a job, right?" I asked him.

"That's right. And he must have been stalking me after I told him there was nothing I could do. We've already discussed this."

"Uh-huh. Was that when you met with him in September, or October, or November, or..."

"What are you getting at Banks?" he asked sharply.

"Oh, I was just trying to square your story with his, that's all," I told him. "I just hate it when things conflict, don't you?"

"What story?" he asked. "Do you mean you've talked to that

183

weasel Maloney recently?"

"Oh, I'm getting to know Victor really well. And everyone he's seen, everyone he knows, everything he's done and who he's done it with. He is just a wealth of very useful information."

"You are so full of shit, Banks. Stop wasting my time," he said, this time more angrily.

"Just one more question. Did you and he do a lot of Christmas shopping together the night of the carjacking?"

"Fuck you, Banks!" he screamed as the line went dead. The burden of the intellectual reply aside, that felt good.

I was still smiling when Sam came back with lunch. She put her lunch and my coffee on the appropriate desks, and looked at me like I had lost my mind. "What did you do while I was out? You look like the cat that ate the canary," she said as she hung up her coat.

"I just got off the phone with Michael Lawrence, whom, as you and I both read in the day planner, allegedly met with Victor Maloney the night of the carjacking. I asked him about it, and instead of a denial or an explanation, I got a 'fuck you'. Pretty cool, huh?"

"So, instead of an explanation, you got verbally abused, and you're okay with that?" she asked, puzzled.

"Well, when you put it that way," I said.

"Or are you trying to say that a rational person would have asked how you knew, where you got your information, or at the very least offered an explanation?"

"Yes I am," I said. I opened the coffee. "Now I need to talk to Maddy Dellaplante about her sister, and we may be able to wrap this up."

Sam took a bite of her sandwich, and wiped her mouth delicately with her napkin before speaking. She may be a shark when it comes to food, but she was a polite and delicate one. "Are you trying to get them riled up?" she asked.

"Uh-huh, and in the process, I hope I can get them to answer some questions without having to ask them directly," I explained.

"You private-eye types are very sneaky, aren't you?"

I simply smiled back and took another swallow of my coffee.

LAKE EFFECT

After we finished lunch I grabbed my coat off the rack and headed out to the hospital.

It turned out to be a nice day for a drive, and if my timing was good I would be getting there right after the nurses finished picking up lunch trays from the patients. That would mean fewer interruptions. Before long I was pulling into the hospital parking lot. As I entered the lobby, I checked to make sure she was still in the same room, and what her condition was. According to the senior citizen volunteer at the desk, she was still in the private room and was listed in critical but stable condition. I asked if there was anyone else in to see her, but the elderly gentleman was of little help.

I took the elevator up to her floor, and proceeded down the hallway. I was hoping Maddy was there, since I knew Frank would be at the zoning board meeting with Lawrence. My luck was holding, as I stood at the doorway and watched as Maddy sat facing her sister's bedside, not speaking. She must have sensed someone was there, because she turned her head to look towards the doorway. "Oh, it's you," she said with a touch of disgust in her voice.

"I get that a lot," I said, with a hint of weariness. "How's your sister doing?"

"She's doing a little better I think," she said in reply.

"That's good. I'm pulling for her."

"Great, I'm sure she'll appreciate it," she said sarcastically.

"Has she regained consciousness?"

"No, not yet."

"Hmmm," I said.

Maddy looked at me again, her eyebrows furrowed. "Mr. Banks, are you here for business or pleasure?" she asked.

"Business, actually. May I talk to you for a few minutes?"

"I'm sure my sister won't be interrupting us. What do you want?" Maddy snapped.

"Well, when I was at Sharon's house with you the day she overdosed, I took the liberty of taking the medicine bottle and water glass she used to take the medicine. I have a friend who works very closely with me in law enforcement, and he managed to get

185

fingerprints off the glass."

"Of course there were fingerprints on the glass. Sharon drank from the glass to wash down her pills. Jesus, you are a lame-ass detective, Banks. You actually had the nerve to steal from my sister's house? I should tell my father to fire you immediately, and demand he report you to whatever agency governs slime balls like you!" she hissed forcefully enough to be heard.

"Her prints weren't on the glass Maddy. Could they be yours?"

"What are you talking about, Banks? Have you lost your God-damned mind?"

"It's so simple, Maddy, even a lame-assed detective like me should be able to figure it out. Sharon never touched the glass, and so she probably never voluntarily drank from it, either. Am I going too fast for you? Do you see where I'm going with this?"

Maddy's eyes started to widen in recognition of what I was saying. I just kept looking at her waiting to see her response to this. After a moment, I stated again. "So Maddy, what I want to know is, and maybe you can help me, what would your fingerprints be doing all over the glass that Sharon used to take the pills she overdosed on?"

She offered no response, just a blank stare in my general direction.

"Let me put it to you another way, Maddy," I said to her. "Is it just possible that you helped her take those pills, all of them?"

Nothing.

"Maddy?"

She snapped out of whatever delirium she was in and glared at me in utter contempt. "If you are trying to accuse me of poisoning my own sister you son of a bitch, so help me I will sue your..."

"Maddy," I said as condescendingly as possible, "I'm not accusing anyone of anything. I just want to make sense of a bad situation, to help you and your family."

"Get out of here right now, Banks. You'll be hearing from my lawyer," she said loudly enough to get the attention of the nurses and hospital security guard on that floor.

"Remember, you will have the right to have that lawyer present during questioning," I informed her as a public service. I put up my

186

LAKE EFFECT

hand to let the nurses and security guy know I was leaving.

"Fuck you, Banks!" she called after me. I smiled again. Two in one day, I thought. I was on a roll.

Thirty-three

Shortly after Banks left, Maddy patted her sister's hand, as if to comfort her. "I'll be right back, Shar," she whispered. As quickly as she could, she walked back down towards the visitor's lounge, to the telephone booth where she had called Lawrence before. She dialed quickly, and when the receptionist answered, she demanded to speak to Michael immediately. Cyndi informed her that he was at a meeting, that he would be back soon, and would she like to leave a message. She did, leaving the phone number at the booth for him to call her back.

She was shaking as she waited for what seemed like hours. She could feel the panic rising from her very core as the annoying silence mocked her own fear. Finally, the phone rang and she startled and jumped. It was Lawrence on the other end of the line.

"Oh God, Michael, he knows," Maddy cried into the phone. "Banks was just here and he knows!"

"Calm down, Maddy," Lawrence told her, controlling his own anger. "Banks doesn't have anything, or he would have brought it to the cops by now. He's just fishing, that's all."

"What makes you so sure he didn't go to the cops already?" she asked, near panic. "He knows Sharon didn't drink from the glass, that I held the glass..."

"Maddy, if you don't relax, you are gonna give everything away. Then what, huh? Think about it," he said harshly.

"I don't want to go to jail, Michael, I don't deserve to go to jail!" she said, fairly shrieking into the telephone. An older couple, who had just come into the lounge shortly after Maddy, stared at her briefly. Maddy made eye contact with them, smiled weakly, then turned away. The couple got up and left the lounge.

"Listen to me carefully, said Lawrence. "I don't want you talking to anyone about anything right now. You are way too crazed to make sense to anybody."

"You bet your ass I'm crazed!" she exclaimed. "Michael, don't you get it? They are going to lock us up, throw away the key, and never let us out! It's over. Banks figured it out, and it's all over," she said hysterically.

"I don't know what line he hit you with, but he called me with this bullshit about talking to Maloney, how he told him that I was at the mall the night of the carjacking, crazy stuff like that. We both know he didn't talk to ol' Victor, so he's gotta be jackin' us to see what we do."

"I don't think so," she said. "My father says Banks is..."

"You know, I really don't care what your father's opinion is on anything, Maddy. He's an old man, and he doesn't know everything," he said.

Maddy seethed on the other end of the line. "You arrogant prick! If my father thinks this guy is a hard ass, then he is."

It was clear antagonizing her was not going to work, he thought. "Yeah, okay, whatever," he sighed. "Let's not fight about this, baby. We got so much to look forward to once we get all this behind us." If she didn't calm down and relax, she was going to screw everything up.

"What do you mean 'we'? If 'we' wind up in prison, there is no more 'us'."

"That's about enough talk about prison. I told you I'll handle Banks, and I meant it. Leave him to me, and for God's sake, don't panic."

"Okay, I'll try," she said, shaking her head. "I'll call you when I get back from the hospital."

"Okay, and don't worry, I'll handle everything," he said, hanging up on her. Lawrence then reached into his back pocket, and pulled out his wallet. Looking through the assorted pieces of paper and business cards, he pulled out the business card for Banks Investigations. He placed it neatly on the desk beside his yellow note pad, and picked up the phone to dial Banks' number.

"Banks Investigations," answered Sam.

"May I speak to Mr. Banks, please?" Lawrence asked.

"I'm sorry, he's not in. I do expect him back later, though. May I take a message?"

LAKE EFFECT

"Just let him know Michael Lawrence called, and I'll be stopping by late this afternoon. About what time do you expect him?"

"I expect him back before 3:30."

"Great. I'll try to catch him before the end of the day. Thanks," he said, hanging up.

Just as Sam hung up the phone, it rang again. Twice in one afternoon, she thought, how will I ever finish this crossword puzzle? "Banks Investigations," she said.

"This is Maddy Dellaplante, is he in?" she asked abruptly.

What a bitch, Sam thought. "No he isn't, is there a message, Miss Dellaplante?"

"How the hell long does it take to get from the hospital to your pitiful little office? Never mind, just tell him I need to see him, and that I'll be coming by on my way home from the hospital. It is very, very important. Is that clear?"

"What's clear is that you need to relax, maybe get a hobby, but I'll tell Joe when he gets in. I expect him soon." The conversation ended abruptly with a rude click on the other end. This is going to get interesting, Sam said to herself as she put away the crossword puzzle.

Thirty-four

I got back to the office, and was promptly greeted by my investigative assistant, doing her best cat-that-ate-the-canary grin. "What did you do?" I asked her quizzically.

"You are going to have a hell of an afternoon. Guess who's coming to see you," she said with that same smile on her face.

"Well, let's see. Gilligan and Skipper are still on their three hour tour, and that actress still won't return my phone calls, so I have no idea. Unless you mean Jimmy Ramone, who wants the day planner Maloney's father sent me."

"Him, too. And...," she teased.

"And? What do you mean and?" I asked.

"And while you were out, Michael Lawrence called. He'll be stopping by a bit later."

"That is a surprise. Anyone else?"

"Of course. Maddy Dellaplante, stopping by on her way home from the hospital." Sam continued to look completely amused.

"You're right, it's beginning to sound like a party. We don't have time for a caterer, maybe we should just send out for pizza and beer."

"Is that all you think about, eating?" she asked.

"Eating, beer, sex, coffee. Yup, that about covers it. And before you ask, no, I never get them confused."

"I wasn't gonna ask."

I checked my gun, and chambered a round before setting the safety. I didn't think that either of them would actually try anything, but I would hate to be wrong, especially in regards to Lawrence. I thought about putting it on the little shelf under the desktop, something I built in for just such an occasion. Instead, I kept it in its holster, visible, as a deterrent. On the shelf I placed a cassette recorder with a fresh tape. When I was satisfied, I opted to call Paula to let her know I had some late appointments and not to hold dinner, just in case.

It was no more than 15 minutes after when Maddy Dellaplante burst through the door like a winter squall, cold and blustery. She glared at Sam, who smiled back at her sweetly. Maddy then turned her attention on me. I hit the record button on the tape player, stood and walked around to the front of my desk as she took off her coat. I leaned back and beckoned her to sit in one of the two wooden chairs I keep for client conferences. She wore a pair of dark blue jeans, a black turtleneck sweater, with black high-heeled boots. Her hair was pulled back in a loose ponytail, revealing a pair of gold hoop earrings and a second pair of diamond studs in each ear. Ms. Dellaplante was fashionably casual in her dress, and distressed in her demeanor. She sat, I leaned, as we talked.

"Joe," Maddy started, "I don't know if your Kelly girl over there told you, but I need to talk to you. It's very important." She motioned to Sam, who was sitting back at her desk, enjoying the show.

"Actually, Miss Kelly," I said for emphasis, "told me all about your call. What's the problem Maddy?"

"I think I know who killed my sister's children, and who may have tried to make it look Sharon committed suicide."

"If you do Maddy, why not take it to the police. They are more than willing to talk to fine, upstanding citizens like you who can give them solid leads."

"I think you know why I'm coming to you. Do we have to talk in front of her?"

"I trust her, and you can, too, if you're being straight with me." I shot Sam a wink, and she nodded in acknowledgement of my confidence in her.

Maddy nodded her acceptance, and continued. "Michael Lawrence, he's the one that killed David and Sarah, and he got that Victor Maloney to help him."

"Okay," I said, heaving a sigh. "Let's run down the list. Why would he do it?"

"He had Sharon wrapped around his finger, and she would do anything for him. He figured with the insurance money, he could talk her into giving it to him and he'd payoff his gambling debts." Her eyes traveled nervously around the room as she spoke. Her version of the relationship didn't jive with Sharon's, but I let her go

LAKE EFFECT

on.

"He used her prescription for Elavil to put the kids to sleep. He didn't want them to suffer, but he still wanted the insurance money. After, while Sharon was still grieving, he told me he was in love with me, and we should get rid of Sharon so we can be together. We saw each other a few times before, behind Sharon's back, but nothing serious. I mean, I had no intention of stealing my sister's man. He told me he didn't love Sharon, and hadn't for a long time, but stayed around because of the children."

"So the whole thing was Lawrence's idea?" I asked her. "Kind of drastic just to pay off some debts, don't you think?"

"Oh, yes," she said excitedly. "But you have no idea how cruel he can be! I've been close to him since then, and he has no regard at all for anyone but himself. It was his idea to force Sharon to take the whole bottle of medicine, hoping she would overdose. Then she would be out of the way and he could have me to himself."

"You let him poison your sister?" Sam piped up from her desk across the room. I looked over at her, and she was shaking her head.

"You don't understand," Maddy said to Sam. Then she turned to me. "I loved him, too, but I was also frightened of him. I had seen his dark side. I knew what he was capable of."

"Alright," I said. "So I still don't know why you've come to me with this?"

"You can help me, Joe," she said plaintively. "You can talk to the cops, tell them that I am willing to help them." She bowed her head and put her hands to her face.

There was a knock on the door, and then it opened as Michael Lawrence came into the office. "Banks," he called as he stepped through the door. "I want to talk to…"

At first he looked at Sam, who smiled and pointed towards Maddy and I.

"Michael," I said, "what a surprise! We were just talking about you."

"Maddy? What are you doing here?" Lawrence asked, ignoring my warm welcome.

"She's decided that she knows a little bit more about the death of her niece and nephew than she thought she did. Didn't you Maddy?" I said, smiling.

"What did she tell you, Banks?" he asked suspiciously. "Maddy, What did you tell him?"

"Oh, Michael," she said, her voice cracking. "I love you, but I couldn't let you get away with what you did to Sharon and her kids. It's not your fault. I understand that now. You're sick, you need help, and they can help you in prison."

"Help me in prison?" he shouted. "You twisted, manipulative bitch! This was all your idea!" Sam and I looked at each other with eyebrows raised. The party was just getting interesting.

"Don't you remember, Michael, you came to me with this plot to kill David and Sarah for the insurance money, and to do the same thing to Sharon so we could be together?" she pleaded with him. Her voice was strained, choking on her own tears. All in all, it was a good show so far.

"What are you talking about?" he shrieked. He turned to me in a panic. "She's lying. Maddy came to me with this plot to get rid of Sharon and the kids to get her dear old Daddy's attention. She told me I could use the money to pay off some gambling debts, and she could forge Sharon's name on the check. All she wanted was to be Daddy's little girl, like Sharon."

"Joe, please listen to me," Maddy said. "He's obviously pathologic in his lying. He needs help. I did what I did, and I'm not proud of it, but I'm willing to help if Michael gets the help he needs."

"I don't believe you!" Lawrence said, stepping closer. I uncrossed my arms, making the holster a bit more visible. It worked. He stopped dead in his tracks, staring at the holster, then at me. "Look, can't you see what's happening here, Banks? She's afraid of going down alone so she's trying to take me down with her."

"Oh, I know. But it's kinda like passing a wreck on the Thruway," I explained. "You know it's morbid, but you gotta slow down to see what happened."

Lawrence's face got beet red, made worse by his fair complexion.

LAKE EFFECT

There was an expression of mixed fear and rage on his face. It made me nervous enough to cross my arms again, in case I had to reach the gun suddenly. In my mind I was praying I wouldn't have to. I looked at Sam, worried how she was doing. She was looking out the opened door. As I caught her eye, she looked at me and nodded slightly.

And then Lawrence did something I truly didn't expect. He started to laugh. It wasn't a nervous laugh, but the laugh of a man who was just tricked and was trying to be a good sport about it. "I've got to hand it to you, Banks," he chuckled. "You're good, you are very good. So what are you going to do now? Call the cops?"

"I don't know, probably not," I said. "I'm really curious to hear what you have to say, since Maddy already sold you out. And whatever happened to Victor?"

"Victor? You don't have to worry about Victor breaking into your house again. I've taken care of that for you."

"Like you took care of David and Sarah?" I asked him calmly.

"Did Maddy tell you that?" Lawrence looked directly at Maddy. "Darling, please, you don't give yourself near enough credit. You planned that the night you decided to use your body on me as a seductive weapon against your sister. And you were very, very persuasive." He was grinning at her. For her part, Maddy shook her head, looking down at her feet.

"Now don't be modest, lover," he said again. "You are the consummate whore. And when you stop and think about it, it really was just business between us. You gave me what I wanted, and I gave you what you wanted."

That's when Maddy leaped to her feet and lunged at Lawrence, her nails digging in to his cheek. As the blood ran down the side of his face, he grabbed Maddy's throat with his right hand as she fell forward. In one move, he gripped tightly and squeezed. His fingers blanched the skin on her neck, his eyes open wide as he tried to choke the life out of her. I moved quickly, and reaching his hand I grabbed the thumb and bent it back hard. He released his grip on Maddy's throat and she fell to the floor coughing. I held his thumb and applied as much pressure as I could to move him away from her.

RONALD W. ADAMS

I felt a pop, then a snap, and Lawrence let out a scream as he grabbed his right hand with his left. As I let go, Ramone walked through the door.

"What were you waiting for?" Sam asked him, moving over to Maddy.

"In crime fighting, as in life, timing is everything," he explained. He walked over to me, shaking his head. "What were you waiting for?" Ramone asked me.

"I had it under control the whole time," I told him, over the pathetic cries of Lawrence. He was still standing, but doubled over gripping his grossly misshapen thumb.

"What are you whining about?" Ramone asked Michael, patting him down and finding a small .22 caliber pistol in his right coat pocket. He showed it to me, and then placed it in his own pocket. Ramone put Lawrence's hands behind his back and snapped a pair of handcuffs on him. "It's still attached, sort of."

"That's gonna hurt when he sits in the back of your car, you know that," I said.

"The price you pay," he said, as he stood Lawrence up. "I need another pair of cuffs, Lucky. Got some?"

I looked at Sam with a questioning look. She shook her head and went to the top drawer of the filing cabinet, pulling out my old pair of handcuffs. She returned to Maddy and ran her hands over the still dazed woman, checking for any weapons. Sam then put Maddy's hands behind her back, and snapped the cuffs on in expert fashion. Ramone watched in awe.

"I think I'm in love," he said slack jawed.

"Get in line," Sam said, smiling and winking at him. I went to my desk and hit the stop and eject buttons on the tape player. I put the cassette on top of the day planner, and handed them both to Ramone.

She looked at me and said, "You'd be lost without me."

"That's exactly what Paula tells me," I said.

198

Thirty-five

I was late for dinner, pretty much as usual. Paula was heavily involved in arts and crafts, today consisting of making paper plate masks for Kyle and Amanda to play with. For a long time I vowed to get rid of the craft and garden channel from our satellite TV service. But Paula refused to let me, and now I see the wisdom of her ways. She loved doing things like that with the kids, and they positively ate up the attention she lavished on them.

I peeled the foil paper off the plate, and put it in the microwave to heat up. I was still on an adrenaline high from the activity at office, and was having a little trouble concentrating when Paula snuck up behind me and kissed me on the ear.

"You all right?" she asked, rubbing my shoulder.

"Yeah. Sorry I'm a little distracted," I told her.

"I know. Sam called and told me basically what happened. You are lucky, you know that."

"I know." I pulled her closer, wrapping my arms around her waist and letting myself get lost in those beautiful eyes. We kissed softly, tenderly, until we were rudely interrupted by the shrill beep of the microwave.

"Eat, and I'll keep the kids off your back for a while," she told me. "We can pick this up again later."

I took the plate to the kitchen table, along with a fork and a bottle of Sam Adams beer. About three bites into a re-heated meal of chicken, mashed potatoes, and peas, Kyle came flying into the room and proceeded to grab my leg in a bear hug. He grinned his handsome, toothy grin at me, blue eyes sparkling and full of fun. Dinner could wait, and I picked him up on to my lap and hugged him tightly.

"Hi, Dadda," he said, still smiling.

"Hi, Buddy," I said to him, kissing his forehead. "I missed you today."

"Yeah, me too. You catch bad guys today?"

"Yeah, I did."

"Like Batman?" he asked with wide-eyed innocence.

"Just like Batman," I told him with a wink.

"Manda!" he shouted, jumping off my lap. "Dadda catch bad guys like Batman!"

Paula looked past the streaking toddler back at me, smiled, and went back to work on a mask with Amanda. I turned back to my dinner, finished it and the beer, and took my plate to the sink to clean up. I rinsed the plate, much to the surprise of my stunned wife, and was about to put it in the dishwasher when a small tug on my pants caught my attention.

"Dadda, got a 'prise for you," Amanda said, her dark brown eyes shining, so much like her mother.

I crouched down to her level. "A surprise for me? Really?" I asked her enthusiastically.

"Yeah," she answered, smiling broadly. "Ta-da!"

She pulled the mask she made with her mom out from behind her back and presented it to me. "A hero mask, like Batman," she explained earnestly.

I sniffled a little, and wiped the beginnings of a tear from my eye, and hugged her tightly. "That's the best surprise I have had all day, baby girl," I told her.

"Love you, Dadda."

"Love you, too, Manda," I said, kissing her cheek.

She ran off to the family room with Paula and Kyle, and I hung the mask in a place of honor on the refrigerator. Soon after, Paula and I put the kids to bed, and finally settled down to talk. The sounds of bed sheets rustling through the baby monitors as the kids settled down to sleep mixed softly with the television.

"Did you get to talk to Frank Dellaplante?" Paula asked, holding my hand as we sat on the couch.

"I called him after we put Lawrence and his daughter in Jimmy's car. I felt like I owed him a heads-up before he got the call from the station or her attorney," I explained to her. "He was truly pissed off, and I expected that. Then he got quiet on me, and finally thanked me for the help. I gave him directions to the police station. I don't

LAKE EFFECT

think he'll let Maddy spend the night there."

"Did he say how his other daughter, Sharon is doing?"

"Better, he said. I don't know if she's aware of what her sister, or Lawrence, did. I'll call tomorrow and give Frank the name of that counselor friend of mine, Phil Carroll. He's a good guy, and he's a very good therapist. It seems to me they will have some things to work through before they can put this behind them."

"I'm sure. It can't be easy to find out your daughters are the feminist Cain and Abel. Any idea what happened to our burglar?" Paula asked, inching closer. She wore the perfume of fried chicken and school paste, and it may as well have been Halston. She made either scent smell sexy.

"He's dead, I'm pretty sure. Neither Maddy nor Michael said it directly, but Lawrence implied that he 'took care' of him. In any event, this won't end well for Victor's father."

"How are you doing with this stuff? Are you okay?" Paula asked, her concern almost palpable in the air between us. She rubbed the back of my shoulders affectionately, and I was ready to give her all day to stop.

"I'm okay, but I feel bad for old man Dellaplante and for John Maloney. If those were my kids, I don't know how I would handle it. I can only hope we are doing a better job of parenting than they did, but is that enough?" I asked rhetorically.

"Time will tell," she said, flooring me with her folksy wisdom. And her unnerving honesty.

"That was supposed to ease my mind? That little tidbit was supposed to make me feel better?" I asked her, turning to face her as we sat.

"Nope," she said with a smile, "this is." She pulled my face gently to hers, and kissed me deeply. I found myself melting, like every time before.

Time will tell.

Epilogue

The mild winter finally gave way to a mild spring. The sun was warming everything, and the days were getting steadily longer. The ice on the lakeshore was disappearing, making it easier to get down to the shoreline to cast. Herbie and Mickey continued going to their favorite spot, fair weather or foul, to keep their tradition alive in memory of Casey. Even now, months after his funeral, they felt the need to keep Casey with them in spirit.

So it was that both men were walking down the ramp to the boat launch by Locksley Park, carrying their poles, creels, and buckets. An early morning chill ensured they kept their fingerless gloves on. That crazy detective, Banks, paid for Casey's grave marker, so Mickey and Herbie were able to scrape together enough cash to put a plaque near their favorite fishing spot as well. Mickey took it out of his back pocket, along with a small hammer and a couple of nails from his coat. Herbie had found a suitable piece of driftwood, Mickey nailed the plaque to it, and the two men placed the memorial above the high water mark on the rocks overlooking the beach. They stood silent for a moment, then proceeded carefully back down to the sand.

They reached the water's edge, and in an almost practiced, choreographed unison they each took a six pack of Old Milwaukee beer out of the buckets they carried, flipped the buckets over, and took a few steps forward. Mickey cast his line out first, sending the bait and sinker well out into the gentle surf. Herbie followed suit, and the two men stepped back and sat on the overturned buckets. Mickey reached down and popped the top on the first can and handed it to Herbie before getting one for him. No words were spoken between them, and they understood what was being said in the other's silence.

They alternated between casting, drinking, and smoking for the majority of the morning. Mickey was watching the horizon, when he noticed Herbie's line drifting to the west towards his own. He tugged sharply on Herbie's sleeve and pointed it out. Herbie yanked on the line, felt the weight on the other end, but nothing fighting. He

LAKE EFFECT

started reeling in, convinced he just caught some kind of lake debris. He pulled and reeled until finally whatever it was came close enough to lift out of the water.

It was a black jacket, with the new Sabres logo on the front, a ripped sleeve, and four small holes in the chest. Herbie dragged it out of the water and held it up. Mickey looked it over very closely, his face darkening as he thought back over the winter. He took the coat off the hook carefully, not wanting to ruin the hook. He carried it back up the ramp, and dumped it into the trash barrel. He walked back to where Herbie was standing, and grabbed the last two beers they brought. He opened them, and handed one to his friend.

"To Casey," said Mickey, his voice breaking as he lifted the can.

"To Casey," said Herbie.

Printed in the United States
16963LVS00001B/337-345